The Developer and The Diva

Alexia Adams

Copyright

The Developer and The Diva
By Alexia Adams
Copyright 2019 by Alexia Adams

Published by:
Alexia Adams
Suite 377
255 Newport Drive
Port Moody, BC V3H 5H1
Canada

Contact: Alexia@alexia-adams.com
www.alexia-adams.com

Edited by Julie Sturgeon and Amanda Bidnall, PhD
Cover design by Steven Novak

Ebook ISBN 978-1-9991756-1-0
Print ISBN 978-1-7774201-1-6

First Electronic Edition August 2019
First Print Edition December 2020

Product of Canada

Dedication

I dedicate this book to Stacey P. Your support and encouragement mean the world to me. Thank you.

Chapter One

Eduardo glanced out the window as the car crawled towards its destination. Multicolored tin-clad buildings, for which this barrio was famous, assaulted his eyes. Tourists from around the world flocked to take selfies in front of them. They considered them 'quaint.' All he saw was poverty and a past he'd give almost anything to erase.

He checked his watch, clenching his teeth. At this speed, the meeting would be over before he even got there.

"Sorry, *Señor* Forenza. The traffic is crazy," Raul said. It didn't matter how many times Eduardo asked to be addressed by his first name. As soon as he was behind the wheel, his driver insisted on formality. "It would be quicker if you walked."

Quicker, but sweatier. And he wanted—no, needed—to project an ice-cold, heart-of-steel image to the protesters who, he'd been warned, were about to wreak havoc on his carefully constructed development schedule. It was his first project since becoming full partner in Alva-Suarez Developments, and he was going to do everything in his power to ensure it went off without a hitch. His reputation was on the line.

Nothing threatened his hard-earned reputation.

Whatever celebrity had been hired to influence the planning meeting was in for a surprise. He'd grown up on the streets of La Boca. He'd dodged thugs in the dark alleys and sold papayas on the street as a child to earn food money. He wasn't a born-rich kid who'd never set foot in one of Buenos Aires's rougher barrios. He wasn't going to be intimidated by some big shot who'd never felt the sharp bite of hunger in the night.

Up ahead, a group of teenagers spilled from the sidewalk onto the road, and the slow crawl of the traffic came to a complete stop. Blaring car horns clashed with the tango music booming from a dance studio on the corner.

"I haven't seen gridlock this bad since the last time Messi played at La Bombonera." Raul punctuated his statement with a long blast of the BMW's horn. Not that the noise made one whit of difference to their progress.

Okay, maybe he'd be slightly flustered if the world-class soccer player showed up at his development meeting. Although a rugby man himself, Eduardo had respect for professional athletes. He personally knew the sacrifices they made to get to the upper echelons in sport.

All the things Eduardo had given up had been for naught—his athletic career had been cut short by an illegal tackle. He rubbed his clavicle and the scars hidden under his shirt. It still ached, mostly during turbulent weather. The surgeon had done an impressive job knitting together his shattered collarbone and repairing his other injuries.

Too bad the doctor hadn't been able to fix the damage done to Eduardo's heart. That pain never went away, no matter the weather. No bad tackle was to blame for it, though, just a self-centered woman who put fame before love. He should have known returning to the community center would bring back memories of her. Good thing it was about to be destroyed.

Suddenly, the vehicle was too confining. "I'll walk. I know a shortcut," Eduardo said. "Wait on Calle Parker. I'll call you when I'm done."

"*Sí, señor.*"

Before Eduardo was even out of the BMW, Raul had shed his jacket and rolled up his sleeves to show his muscles and tattoos. The luxury car would be a target in this area, but he was a match for any trouble he might face.

Eduardo shrugged out of his own suit jacket while keeping a tight grip on his briefcase. As he walked, he scanned the faces of those heading towards the community center. Few were wearing Messi, Barcelona, or Boca Junior jerseys, so maybe this wasn't going to be his fanboy dream day.

The entrance to the community center was packed with people. Two security guards stood by the door, their eyes darting around, fists clenched on the truncheons hanging from their belts. It would take at least ten minutes—time he didn't have—to even make it to the door. Hopefully, other members of the planning committee were already inside. If the meeting had to be rescheduled because some VIP's presence prevented a quorum, he'd seriously lose his shit. They were already up against cascading deadlines.

Thankfully, he knew where the back entrance was

located, having spent a great deal of his youth either trying to get in, or out, of the center.

He slipped into the building. The custodian let him pass. Either he didn't recognize Eduardo, or the tailor-made suit and Italian leather shoes were enough to legitimize the kid who'd been one step from the wrong side of the law for most of his youth.

The meeting was to be held in the gymnasium, so he headed in that direction. The hallway still had the same chipped brown floor tiles and scratched, dented, and graffiti-marred yellowish walls. If he looked, he'd probably find his own contribution: *E+A para siempre* inside a badly drawn heart. He didn't look. Graffiti lied. Forever? What a joke. They'd barely lasted three years.

The closer he got to the gym, the stronger the scent of cleaning fluid, rubber, and sweat. One look should be enough to convince the committee that this place needed to be torn down. His plan for a mid-rise apartment building with retail space on the ground floor was a much better use for this land. Who hung around a community center these days? Kids were either on their phones or playing video games. Senior citizens, too, for that matter.

He paused outside the door to put on his game face. Damn memories. His palms were clammy, and his stomach had taken up freediving. The sooner this place was demolished, the better.

Feedback from a microphone inside the room halted the excited chatter for a nanosecond. Then the muffled voice of the chairperson could be heard through the door. Nothing like making a last-minute entrance. Eduardo pushed open both doors and strode through, halting two steps into the room, as that was all the space available. There had to be twice as many occupants as legally allowed. Behind the rows of folding chairs, people stood six deep.

Eduardo's eyes roved the crowd as he pressed his way forward as politely as possible. With so many bodies in the way, he couldn't see who the star attraction was. Because he was damn sure these people hadn't turned up at ten o'clock on a Monday morning to hear a dry recitation of the planning application under consideration.

He was two meters from the tables set up between a battered podium at the front of the room before he could see who had caused the mayhem.

His heart stalled. Then it joined his stomach in a race to see which would make it to his knees first. Staring back at him, as shocked as he was, was the *A* in *E+A forever.*

Excellent. This demolition wouldn't even require a wrecking ball.

***

Frank Sinatra had done things his way with a few regrets. Anna had only the one. But it was a doozy—and it had just walked into the room.

Her heart pounded so loudly she was sure the microphone would pick it up and broadcast her distress to the entire audience. It'd been torture enough walking through the halls of the building that held so many of her most treasured memories: her first kiss, her first dance, and the moment when her heart had switched ownership, only to be thrown back at her three years later with permanent cleat marks embedded in it.

The co-owner of those memories, and the guy who'd trampled her racing organ, was walking towards her, looking like he'd slice her to pieces given the opportunity.

And she couldn't really blame him. She'd burned their relationship to the ground. Then she'd flung the ashes to the wind and made a million dollars. Several million, actually.

However, if Eduardo hadn't been so pigheaded, arrogant, and, well … macho, maybe they'd have had a different ending. Or no ending. And she wouldn't be faced with her current dilemma.

Now *there* was a thought to make her squirm in her chair.

That was an issue for another day. This instant, her focus was on why Eduardo would show up here now. Was he about to denounce her as a fraud, as a woman who sang of love but was incapable of the emotion? He'd be wrong.

Maybe he was another 'celebrity' here to lend his support to the opposition, hoping to halt the destruction of a neighborhood landmark. His rugby career had been incredibly short, but he'd been hailed as a national hero when he'd scored the winning try in Argentina's one and only victory over New Zealand's All Blacks. Was he still riding that claim to fame? Surprisingly—or not, given the way they'd ended—he'd never cashed in on his role as her first boyfriend.

Looking at him now, *boyfriend* was not the word that came to mind. *Madre de Dios*, he'd become a stunning man. He'd always been taller than most, his shoulders and chest strong enough to give her respite from all her fears. Now they were even more magnificent. He might no longer be a professional athlete, but he clearly hadn't stopped his fitness routine. Desire trampled regret in its bid to be the overwhelming emotion of the moment.

She shifted in her chair. Eduardo would take the empty seat next to hers. Long-suppressed memories surfaced of his muscled thighs pressed against hers, and her skin warmed. With her pale coloring, soon everyone in the room would know she wanted him.

The blood that had moments ago flushed her cheeks receded like a cockroach in the light when Eduardo took a chair at the opposite table. What? He wanted to destroy this place? Their gazes met for a split second and she audibly caught her breath at the loathing she saw in his mocha brown eyes. He definitely hadn't forgiven her.

Thankfully, at that moment, the chairperson called the meeting to order. Marshaling every ounce of willpower she possessed, Anna channeled her nervous energy into presenting the image for which she was famous: an ethereal beauty untouched by the world's woes.

What a load of bullshit.

Surreptitiously, she texted her assistant, instructing Janet to send her everything known about Eduardo Forenza, especially over the past five years. When Anna had first gone to LA, she'd cyberstalked Eduardo, desperate to know if he'd made a full recovery from his career-ending injury. But since he was no longer in the world of professional athletes, there had been little information on the web. He'd always been private and, as far as she'd been able to discover, he never had any social media accounts.

For her sanity, she'd stopped searching for word about him. She'd given up all contact with any friends who'd known them as a couple. Eduardo was her past. She'd moved on. Sort of.

The dry recitation of the planning application over, the chairperson called on the developer's representative to expound on the benefits his proposed new building would bring to the community.

Without sparing even a glance in her direction, Eduardo strode to the lectern. At last, she had an excuse to stare at him. His voice was deeper now than she remembered, coming from the depths of his soul, offering shelter and sanctuary.

But not to her. Not anymore.

His dark-brown hair was cut short. Too short. It used to curl against his collar and give her something to hold onto as his lips traced a path from her ear to her shoulder, turning her knees to water. His lips were the same—full, promising endless delight. She'd dreamed about those lips on her body.

His dark, chocolate-colored eyes, which used to soften when she walked into the room, were hard. His steely determination to see his project come to life was evident for all to see. This was a man who knew what he wanted—and stopped at nothing to get it.

A tailor-made suit hugged his lean form, hinting at the amazing body she knew was hidden beneath. Her fingers itched to trace the contours of his back, to feel his chest muscles react to her touch, to hear his whispered words of encouragement as she rubbed her hips against his.

The room got too hot, but she resisted the urge to fan herself. The breath she pulled in was harsh and unsteady.

"Are you okay?" Johanna, the head of the community protest group, leaned over and whispered in Anna's ear.

"Yes," she managed to reply through a throat thick with memories. "Just jet lag hitting me."

The woman patted Anna's knee, a gesture so similar to her grandmother's that a wave of grief threatened to obliterate Anna's tenuous grip on composure.

The chairperson's voice came to her through a haze. "And now we'd like to welcome to the podium the singing sensation Angel. What many of you may not know is that Angel grew up right here in La Boca and spent hours enjoying these facilities."

Great. She'd been so busy staring at Eduardo that she hadn't heard a word he'd said. She'd just have to go with her prepared statement about how the community's youth needed a place to meet, to learn, to develop essential skills. Although she'd done none of those things. Her time here had been spent almost entirely in Eduardo's arms. She probably shouldn't mention that.

It took five minutes for the crowd to quiet down

before she could speak. Like at her concerts, there were those who called out that they loved her, those who started to sing her most popular song, hoping she'd join in, and those who screamed just to make noise. When she glanced to the left, Eduardo sat with his arms crossed over his chest, a glower puckering the skin between his eyebrows. Based on the muscles working in his jaw, his molars were being ground to dust.

She held up her hand and eventually the room quieted. "This community center," she said, pausing to clear her throat, "was witness to some of my happiest days." She didn't dare look at Eduardo but allowed her voice to soften. "It distresses me greatly to think that today's youth won't have a place to gather if this building is destroyed for apartments no one in the area will be able to afford."

Eduardo stood and came around to the front of his table. Even a meter away, she could feel his strength, his determination to sway the committee to his viewpoint. "If Angel," he sneered her stage name, "had listened to my presentation rather than playing on her phone, she'd have realized that 'today's youth' don't 'gather' here anymore. They hang at the park or each other's homes, where they play online games, surf the internet, or watch YouTube videos." His voice carried so well she was sure that the people at the very back of the room could hear him even without the microphone. A general murmur of agreement rose among the crowd.

"And while it's all very nice that she has such fond memories of the place, those of us who still live here, who walk these streets every day, know that what La

Boca needs is safe housing and reasonable-rent commercial space to allow *locals* to conduct business and earn a living to feed and clothe their children. We can't all live in mansions in Beverly Hills and charge twenty thousand pesos for a ticket to one of our concerts."

He perched his delectable ass on the table, stretched his long legs, crossed his ankles, and folded his arms over his abdomen, blatantly challenging her to respond.

As she racked her brain for a counter to his argument, there was a commotion at the back of the room. A deafening *bang* was followed immediately by pandemonium. Most in the audience stood, blocking her view. Chairs crashed to the floor, and a few people screamed.

Before she could even formulate a plan of escape, Eduardo was in front of her, further preventing her from seeing whatever was happening at the door. Without a word, he ushered her towards the curtained area behind them.

Within seconds, they were enveloped in darkness behind the heavy curtain, his body pressed against hers. His heart beat steadily beneath her hand and his scent, a mix of bergamot and sandalwood, suited the man he'd become.

"Where's your security team?" Eduardo's whisper straight in her ear sent heat directly to her core. Damn, but she wished she could turn back time, if only for a few hours. Where was a time-travel rune stone when you needed one? Or did those only work in Scotland?

"I didn't bring any. I thought I'd be safe. This used

to be my home." She'd wanted to just be Anna Marquez for a while. But as the shouts of terrified people grew, she realized the folly of her plan.

There was no going back to a simpler life—one where Eduardo loved her.

Chapter Two

Eduardo forced his brain to recall every exit the community center offered and not dwell on the sensations bombarding him with Anna back in his arms. His body, however, refused to ignore her soft breasts crushed into his chest. Her hands were on his shoulders, his growing erection pressed against her stomach. Just like the good old days. Damn traitorous body. He'd make it pay later with a double workout.

His hand eventually released her hip and searched to the left. He shuffled them over a few feet, making sure they were still covered by the heavy curtain. He prayed that in the confusion no one noticed the bulge in the draperies. There were shouts asking for calm and for everyone to vacate the room in an orderly manner. It had been nothing more than a firecracker that had unleashed the chaos, but he wasn't taking any chances with Anna's life.

His building would never get the green light if one of Argentina's most prosperous exports was killed on the site.

The last thing he needed was for her to become a martyr. And, yes, that was the only reason he was rescuing her.

At last he made contact with a metal handle and held

his breath as he tried the door. It wasn't locked. First good thing to happen to him today. They were about to enter either the ball storage room or the coach's office. He didn't dare turn on the light and alert anyone to their location. Beyond the curtain, people were calling Anna's name—her fake name. They had a minute, maybe two, before they were discovered. He couldn't be the only one who knew all the make-out spots in the building.

In a second stroke of luck, they were in the coach's office, not the windowless ball room. His eyes had now adjusted to the dark and he found the cord for the blinds. With one tug, diffused sunlight flooded the room. He glanced at Anna to make sure she was unhurt.

Dios, she was beautiful. Even after all their years apart she still stole his breath.

Her long, platinum-blonde hair was coiled in an elegant roll at the back of her neck, and her eyes were the color of the blue stripes in the Argentine flag. No wonder she was considered a national treasure. His gaze lingered on her lips. How many hours had he spent tasting them and her soft skin? Kissing her had been the highlight of each day.

His only regret was that they'd never taken things all the way. They'd assumed they had forever. He'd been so naïve.

"Now what?" she asked in a soft whisper. *Mierda*, memories were doing a trick on him. Good thing he was immune to her now.

"Now I get you out of here." He pulled his phone from his pocket and sent a text to Raul to leave the car and hurry to the back alley behind the community center.

And to message him when he was in position.

The high window was too small for him to make it out, but Anna should have no problem. It was the six-foot drop on the other side that would be the issue.

"How?" She glanced towards the window. "You've got to be kidding me."

"It will be fine. My driver will be on the other side to catch you."

"And you?"

"I'll go out the normal way."

Panic widened her blue eyes. "But where will I meet you?"

"You don't need to meet me. Raul will take you to my car and drop you anywhere you want."

He would not cave to her display of anxiety. He'd rescued her, and he would ensure she got to safety—that should be enough.

"But we need to talk."

He rummaged through the desk, looking for anything that could be used as a disguise. She stood out like a peach in a bowl of pinecones. His quest also kept him from succumbing to her sorcery. Years ago, she'd put a spell on him where he'd do absolutely anything just to see her smile.

"Talk? Why? I think your silence over the past decade has been clear enough. After I was injured—and it was evident that I wouldn't be able to provide you immediately with a lavish lifestyle—you left, seeking a more lucrative relationship."

"It wasn't like that." The anguish in her voice was well faked.

"Put this on." He thrust a filthy baseball cap in her hands. He wasn't going to listen to any protest. She slipped on the nasty hat. It did nothing to disguise her beauty. But hopefully, with her signature hair hidden, she would be able to escape unnoticed by the majority.

"Eduardo…" *Dammit.* Five more minutes and he'd never have to see her again. He could last that long.

Ignoring the plea in her voice, he climbed onto the desk, opened the window, and stuck his head out. Remarkably, the alley was empty of people, but he could hear the crowd around the front of the building. How long they'd stay there and not venture to the back, he had no idea.

Hurry, Raul.

While Eduardo was confident that he could keep Anna safe, it was now his own peace of mind that was at the greatest risk.

He spied his driver rounding the corner at full tilt, and Eduardo held out his hand to help Anna onto the desk. She slipped her delicate palm against his, as she had a million times in the past. Their eyes met for a split second before he released her hand and laced his fingers to offer her a boost through the open window. She pulled herself up, balancing for a moment on the ledge as she maneuvered her white-denim-clad legs into the opening. He heard Raul's reassuring "I've got you" through the concrete wall.

Of their own volition, his eyes met Anna's one last time before she slipped from view.

It was going to take days, and more than a double workout, before he would be able to erase from his mind the haunting sadness in her gaze.

***

Anna flashed her fan-favorite smile for Raul. "I promise, I'll take the full brunt of Eduardo's anger. And if he fires you, I'll hire you at twice the salary," she reassured him. She'd refused to divulge where she was staying, and after forty minutes, Raul had given up and brought her to Eduardo's luxury apartment in the Retiro neighborhood's famed Kavanagh building.

"I don't need anyone to plead for me. I will face Señor Forenza for my decision," Raul said. "And I thank you for the offer, but I can't work for you in America. I have a son and am not able to leave Argentina."

Devoted father had not been one of the pegs she'd put on the board.

"How old is your boy?" Anna asked as she wandered over to the balcony and looked out at the view over Plaza San Martin. She'd forgotten how much she loved her birth city. Los Angeles was great, but it didn't have the history or the evocative architecture of Buenos Aires.

What she didn't miss was the day-to-day struggle of living in poverty, wondering each month if she, her mom, and her grandmother would be out on the street if they couldn't scrape together enough money for rent.

"Timoteo is three." Raul pulled out his phone and showed her a photo of a beautiful little boy with light brown hair and green eyes. There wasn't much resemblance to the hulking giant who had lifted her effortlessly from the window and almost carried her to the BMW waiting around the corner. With his crooked nose, scarred and pockmarked face, and both arms covered in tattoos, Raul was a daunting figure. But as he gazed at the picture of his son, all she could see was complete adoration in the man's face.

"Do you have a picture of his mother as well?"

"No. That snake left, and good riddance. She walked out on the two of us and now thinks she can sue me for custody and take Timo away? I'll be dead before I let that happen."

Was this the bond that glued Raul and Eduardo together? The driver seemed to almost worship his employer. Except instead of the hard-working, dedicated father Raul seemed to be, Eduardo's mother had abandoned him with an alcoholic dad and a crippled grandmother.

"Well, your son looks happy, which shows what a great parent you are."

"I'd do anything for him." Raul's face once again turned thoughtful. "Señor Forenza gave me a job when no one else would. I'd do anything for him as well."

"I'm sure he appreciates your loyalty."

She knew exactly how much Eduardo valued that quality. And what he thought of those who betrayed him. As she had done.

Despite her assurances to the contrary, she knew Eduardo wouldn't be happy to find her in his apartment. But she wasn't going anywhere until she'd at least apologized for leaving him all those years ago. Hopefully, he'd give her the chance to explain, but she wasn't holding her breath for that. Getting his forgiveness would never even be an option. But her husband's recent passing had taught Anna that regret ate at the soul as badly as cancer ravaged the body. She didn't want to lie on her deathbed and think of all the things she should have said.

She rehearsed again her opening lines, knowing she'd only get one shot at this. Her throat tightened.

"Can I get a glass of water?" she asked.

"Of course."

She followed Raul into an immaculate kitchen with marble countertops and hidden appliances. The driver opened a cupboard, pulled out a glass, and poured her a drink from a bottle in the fridge.

"It looks like you've been here before."

He handed her the drink. "Timo and I stayed here for a week while there was a problem with our apartment. As I said, I'd do anything for Señor Forenza."

Including throwing an unwanted guest off the balcony? But she had no fear of Eduardo hurting her physically. His hate was punishment enough.

She wandered back into the living room with its high ceiling and honey-toned walls. The dark wood floors contrasted with the overstuffed white sofas. Red accents in the throw cushions and knickknacks added a punch of color and gave the room a homey feel. The furnishings were not only comfortable but of the highest quality. And the artwork that decorated the walls had clearly not come from a department store. Eduardo had done well, even without the salary of a professional athlete.

So much for his words about still walking the streets of La Boca. He was as much of a fraud as Angel.

Her assistant had finally answered the text asking for background info on Eduardo. She'd read the reply six times in the back seat of the BMW, wearing the hoodie Raul had procured to aid in her disguise. All Janet had been able to discover was that Eduardo was one of Buenos Aires's most prosperous lawyers and had recently become a partner in a property development firm.

He was equally successful with women. After the sixth link to photos of him with some supermodel or gorgeous television personality, Anna had stopped looking into his personal life. His active involvement in several charities was not a surprise. He'd always been one to champion the disadvantaged. He'd become a man any woman would give a kidney to be with.

Unlike Keanu Reeves in *The Matrix*, she'd chosen the wrong pill.

A large, tawny cat sauntered down the hallway. It stopped, stared at Anna for a few seconds, then ignored her as it stretched out in a patch of sunlight. Feline and master seemed to share the same opinion of her.

The lock on the door buzzed. She smoothed a hand over her hair and pulled at the wrinkles on her powder blue top, wishing she'd worn a more try-and-ignore-me-now outfit. Except that would have made escaping through the window of the community center impossible, or at least highly embarrassing.

Eduardo strode through the door looking none the worse for having braved a throng of her ardent fans and made his way out of Boca without his private car and driver. His eyes narrowed when he spotted her standing by the window, but his question was directed at Raul.

"What's she doing here?"

"She insisted that she had to speak with you and wouldn't tell me where she was staying."

"You should have just left her in Boca, since evidently that's what she considers home." Eduardo flung his suit jacket on a wingback chair and strode into the kitchen.

She'd give him a minute to settle before launching into her apology. She'd hoped to do it in private, but Raul didn't look like he was going anywhere. At this point, though, she didn't know if his continued presence was due to curiosity or a determination to protect her—or his boss.

Eduardo returned to the sitting room, a glass of water in hand, his tie gone, and his shirtsleeves rolled up to his elbows. Damn the man, was there no reprieve from his sexiness? Her body shrieked that here was an answer to her problem.

"You know I couldn't abandon her there, boss." Raul held his hands out in a pleading gesture, but there was a look of defiance in his eyes.

Eduardo still ignored her, keeping his gaze trained on his driver. "I thought you of all people would be immune to a witch's charms."

Raul's gaze bounced between Eduardo and Anna, clearly trying to figure out what the deal was between them. The antagonism was blatantly about more than just the fate of the community center.

"Have you met her before?"

Instead of replying, Eduardo glanced at his watch. "It's nearly time to pick up Timo. You can go. I'll get rid of my unwelcome guest."

Raul still stared at Eduardo, his mouth open. "You know this is Angel, the superstar singer, don't you?"

"I know exactly who she is. And her name is Anna."

It took a second, but realization dawned. "Ah, she's *Anna* to you." A teasing gleam entered Raul's eyes. "Well, when you drop her off, wear the hat. I left it on the passenger seat."

"You think I'm going to wear a chauffeur's hat? You don't even wear it, and that's your actual job."

Raul shrugged, heading towards the door. "I just thought you might want to disguise yourself a bit. Otherwise, I look forward to tomorrow's headlines: *Buenos Aires's most eligible bachelor seen with Argentina's sweetheart.*

A half smile replaced the tightness in Eduardo's lips. "You're never going to let me forget that eligible bachelor thing, are you?" Maybe she should ask Raul to stay if it kept her former boyfriend in a better mood.

"Not while it still gets a rise out of you. If you need me, give me a call. I can always bring Timo. He, too, loves Angel." The last bit was addressed to her.

She'd fled the community center with only her phone, so she had no publicity photos or anything to send to the little boy. And she was sure Eduardo wouldn't appreciate her flaunting her fame in his face.

Anna had sent a message to Johanna, who'd roped her into the appearance today, to let her know she was safe. Johanna was not only the head of the protest committee but also a friend of the family, so it hadn't taken too much persuasion for Anna to agree to be the famous face of their cause. After the development meeting, they'd planned for Anna to do a signing while gathering signatures to prevent the destruction of the community center.

Had Eduardo known that? He'd been very calm when everyone else around was panicking.

"Did you stage that distraction this morning?"

Eduardo's eyes turned glacial. "You think I'm that underhanded? It shows what kind of people you hang out with now."

Even Raul's eyes had narrowed at her accusation. With a shake of his head, he left.

For the first time in ten years, she was alone with Eduardo.

Goosebumps broke out on her arms, and her heart tried to launch itself out of her chest, aiming for Eduardo's feet. Her mouth was so dry that if she tried to speak, all that would come out would be dust.

She gulped down the rest of the water while Eduardo stood across the room, looking like he was considering whether or not she was too big to be sucked up by his vacuum.

"So, you're BA's most eligible bachelor?" Dammit, that was not how she'd wanted to start this conversation.

"A stupid title I neither want nor need. Why are you here, Anna? I made it abundantly clear at the community center that I never wanted to see you again."

His arms were crossed over his chest, his feet hip-width apart, as though preparing for a fight.

"We need to talk. About the community center," she added when he was about to turn away. She'd have a better chance to fix the past if they sorted out their present conflict first.

He turned back, his brown eyes narrowed.

"Why do you even care what happens to the place? Aside from two concerts, you haven't been back in the country in five years."

He'd kept track of her? Argentina held too many memories, both good and bad, for her to return more frequently. Staying away helped keep her sane.

If it hadn't been for her grandmother's passing, she wouldn't even be here now.

"The community center was such an important part of our lives. It gave us a place to go when home was more of a nightmare than being on the streets." Her mother's constant criticism meant Anna escaped the apartment as often as possible. And helping younger children at the center had given her a purpose she'd sorely lacked in her adolescence.

Eduardo's youth had been worse than hers. His father, when drunk, had been abusive. His grandmother had never had a good word to say about anyone or anything. The community center had been his refuge— a place where he could be himself and dream of a better future. A future that should have included her.

"That's the past," Eduardo said. "Look at the facts. The property has been underused for years and is practically falling down. It's time to redevelop. Housing and commercial space are what Boca needs most now."

"But what if the center was modernized and offered programs that teenagers were interested in taking?"

"There's no money for that. It's not going to happen."

"I have the money—"

"Money, yes. Commitment? No way." She let that jab pass. It was true. She didn't have the time to champion a project like this. "This is not an issue for which you can just write a check. It would mean continual reassessment and adjustment. Plus, the building is in bad shape. It would be cheaper to tear it down and start again rather than repair. We spent a year doing feasibility studies. Our proposal is the best use of the space for the community."

"Can't you use some of the commercial space in your new building for a youth center?"

He ran a hand through his hair. That she felt the tug on her heart wasn't expected. "It's not viable with the current plans. The businesses will suffer if a lot of teenagers are hanging around."

"But—"

"Face it. You have no argument here, Anna. Now, if that's all you have to say, I'd like you to leave."

"Eduardo…" His name came out a husky whisper as her throat clogged with all the things she wanted to say but couldn't.

He didn't even hesitate. "I'll wait for you in the car."

From the set of his shoulders, she knew he took great pride in being the one to walk away this time.

Chapter Three

Eduardo's hand lingered on the stopper to the whisky bottle. He was very aware of the slippery slope that could start with even one drink. He imbibed socially, but whenever he felt he *needed* a drink, he walked away.

He needed one now. But no way in hell would he allow Anna to be the catalyst that led him down the same destructive path his father had taken following his mother's abandonment. He poured himself a large glass of water instead and drank it all. Every muscle in his body ached, having spent hours in the gym earlier, pounding out his frustrations. It hadn't worked. He was still wound tighter than a tourniquet.

How could one tiny woman he'd known a decade ago wreak such havoc on his peace of mind? It had been a youthful infatuation. He should be over her.

Instead, he was pacing his sitting room floor at two in the morning, deliberately keeping his eyes from the window, knowing he could see her hotel from his apartment. Would the lights be on in her suite? Was she too restless to sleep as well? Or had today been nothing more to her than a minor adventure where she'd run into a shadow from the past?

The disappointment in her eyes as he'd dropped her at the back door of her hotel seemed to indicate otherwise.

Did she regret the way she'd ended things between them? He'd been tempted to ask but had been afraid of the answer. It was easier to hold onto the anger and the pain. That's what had galvanized him to become successful. Without that, he was just another guy who worked too much.

Well, he was awake, so he might as well use the time wisely. He powered up his laptop. But before he could put his finger on the ID scanner, his cell phone rang. Unknown caller. He was tempted to let it go to voicemail, but it could be his business partner, Tiago, calling from France.

"Eduardo, a*yúdame*!"

What the hell had happened to Anna now? Alarms blared in the background, making it difficult to hear her.

The hair on the back of his neck stood on end, and he was pulling on his shoes before he'd even ascertained the reason for her call.

"Slow down, Anna. Tell me again. Why do you need my help?"

"The hotel room below mine is on fire. I have to evacuate. I don't have security in place—"

He should have asked her what all this had to do with him. Why, of all the people she knew in BA, had she called him? But he didn't. "I'll meet you where I dropped you off this afternoon."

It seemed the past wasn't finished messing with him yet. Perhaps he could seize this opportunity for closure and ask her the questions that tormented his soul. Maybe then he could find a woman who made him smile like

Vivi did Tiago.

No.

He wasn't ready to risk another mauling to his heart just yet. He'd settle for a semi-casual relationship that lasted more than two months.

Emergency vehicles surrounded the hotel. Hundreds of people loitered across the street behind caution tape. Many were wearing the hotel-supplied bathrobes. He parked two blocks away and made his way around to the staff entrance at the back of the hotel. Uniformed employees leaned nonchalantly against the dumpsters, several taking the opportunity to have a smoke or level up on some game on their phones.

Standing alone with a guitar slung over the back, a hoodie-clad figure had arms crossed over their chest—to keep warm or warn people away, he wasn't sure. His body knew exactly who was attempting a disguise.

Anna was safe. So why did his stupid pulse accelerate? He didn't even want to see her.

Yet here he was.

She raised her face as he approached. The years melted away. Muscle memory was to blame when he wrapped his arms around her as he'd done too often to forget anytime this century. Her whole body trembled. "It's okay. I've got you," he said against the top of her head, where his lips had no business being. He released her before he did something stupid. Like kiss her.

Dios, he wanted to kiss her. More than he'd wanted that drink.

He ushered her towards his vehicle, not saying another word. In addition to her hair, which he was glad she'd hidden, her speaking voice was distinctive. Hundreds of people had been drawn to the fire. If they knew a celebrity was in their midst, he could only imagine the stampede. He did not need to add a mobbing to his day.

They made it safely to his BMW, but taking her back to his place was the last resort. It'd been bad enough when she'd been there earlier. He did not need his sanctuary destroyed by insidious memories of her.

Did she still have family here who could take her in?

He unlocked the car and opened the passenger door for her. "I was sorry to hear about your *abuela*," he said. Of all the people he would never see again after Anna's departure, her grandmother was the one he missed the most. She'd been a grand lady in every sense of the word.

"Thank you. How did you know?" she asked after he'd taken up his position behind the steering wheel.

"You aren't scheduled for a concert, and I seriously doubt the community center was inducement enough for you to visit. I asked my assistant to check for any notices regarding your family. She found the obituary in Wednesday's paper. It made no mention of you."

"Because it was a tribute to Abuela. She was always my biggest fan, but I didn't want to make her passing about me."

He nodded. If others made the connection, the funeral would turn into a circus. "You have my sympathy. She was an amazing lady. She was..." He didn't want to open up to Anna. But he also knew the pain of having no one to share grief with. Despite the past, he couldn't let her go through that alone. "Your abuela was the first person to show me what real love looked like."

"Excuse me?"

"The way she cared for you. It was real love. I didn't have that at home. My father loved me, but he loved a drink more. My grandmother loved being right above everything. But your abuela... Like I said, she was amazing. When I would come over for dinner, sometimes I'd just listen to the two of you talk about nothing. I promised myself that one day I'd have that too."

"Someone to talk about nothing with?"

"Someone who cared about even the little things in my life, like a funny sign I saw or an odd occurrence. Your dinners, they were the conversational equivalent of a hug—warm and loving. I envied your relationship with her. To me, with my miserable home life, she was the embodiment of family."

"She liked you too."

Well, she'd been the only one of Anna's family who had. The rest thought he was a no-good loser who would just bring her heartache. How wrong they'd been about that.

A chill slithered down his spine. "Is your mother here as well?"

"No." Her curt tone indicated the end of the discussion.

He hadn't started the car, not sure yet where he would take her. "Where's your security team? Your entourage? I thought you pop stars traveled with a supporting army."

"They're all back in LA. I'm here alone. I haven't had a new song out in more than three years. I haven't toured in almost two. My record label is telling me I'm in danger of being forgotten. Just for two weeks I wanted to be … *me*. The me I was before I became *her*."

She spoke like Angel was another person. And not one she particularly cared for at the moment. Fame clearly came at a price—it cost more than just their love.

Of more immediate concern, however, was what to do with her. "Anna, fifty years could pass after you released your last song and the people of Argentina would still remember you. You're the girl who made good on your dreams. You're an inspiration."

"I don't feel like one right now."

He wiped a hand across his eyes. "It's late. It's been an eventful day. You're probably exhausted. A good sleep, and tomorrow you'll be ready to take on the world again."

"Undoubtedly." There was hesitation in her tone.

But she'd bounce back. She always had after a disappointment. As a teenager, her cheery nature had brought sunshine into the lives of everyone she came across. Tomorrow she'd return to being a diva and he'd be relegated once more to the past.

His finger hovered over the engine start button.

"Do you have any family or friends left here who could put you up for the night?"

"Not really." A bitter laugh escaped her. "Eighteen-year-old me was very good at burning bridges. I could ask one of my grandmother's friends…"

They wouldn't be able to keep her safe. But sitting in these bucket seats all night wasn't an option either. He pulled in a deep breath then started the car. It looked like he wouldn't be eradicating her from his soul just yet. He could always move if the memories got too intense.

Within minutes, they were ensconced in his apartment. This time he didn't hesitate at the whisky bottle. He poured them both a generous drink.

What now?

He should usher her to a guest room, say good night, and leave for work in the morning before she got up.

Instead he handed her the glass, careful to avoid touching her.

Where was his pride? Where was his logic?

"You've had quite the day," he said.

She sipped the whisky, a frown marring her brow. "You don't think the two incidences are related, do you?"

He studied her face. Could they be connected? He'd check with a police officer friend tomorrow. But for tonight he needed her reassured … and out of his sight. "I don't see how. The community center thing was just some stupid kid trying to scare a bunch of adults and maybe get close to you. And we don't know what caused the fire. It could have been a careless person smoking in bed and falling asleep."

She nodded. "I guess."

He slung back the whisky, enjoying the sensation as it slid down his throat. It was nice for a different part of his body to burn. His chest had taken enough hits today.

"There's a guest suite, first door on the right. It should have everything you need for the night." He would not think about her sleeping meters from his bed. Especially naked. Nope, that would be stupid.

She moved towards the hallway then stopped. Tears streamed down her cheeks.

"You're safe here," he said. His arms ached to hold her. Just one more time. But he was stronger than that desire. At least for now.

"It's not that. I..." She pulled in a deep breath. "Edio..." His old nickname, one she'd only used when they kissed, sliced his heart to ribbons. "I made the biggest mistake of my life when I left you. There's not a day that goes by that I don't regret it. I just ... wanted you to know."

Those were the words he'd needed to hear since forever. Too bad they didn't bring the relief he expected. His fingers tightened on the glass in his hand. If it wasn't lead crystal, it probably would have shattered. "Well, the sacrifice paid off for you. You're famous. Millions of people adore you. You're Angel."

"I only wanted to be *your* angel. Do you remember? You used to call me that: *mi ángel*."

Yes, he remembered. Dios, he wished he didn't.

"Use any room. I'm going to stay at a friend's place."

He left while he still could.

***

Anna straightened her legs on the sofa, dislodging a pile

of crumpled manuscript paper covered with scratched-out lyrics and music notes. If she didn't write some songs soon, she would be forgotten. Perhaps not in Argentina, but in the rest of the world.

She'd considered putting out an album of covers or maybe doing a collaboration with up-and-coming artists. But she'd floated those ideas to her record label's management to only a lukewarm response. They wanted Angel originals. The stuff that put the *ching* in *cha-ching*.

They'd made allowances for her disappearance from the public eye for the six months following her husband's death. But now the monthly calls were weekly calls, asking when she'd be returning to work. She had one more album on her contract, and it was already late. They wouldn't wait much longer. There were a thousand potential Angels, all vying for their shot at the stars.

She was on the verge of irrelevancy.

Everything she'd given up would be for naught.

Unless she tried to get it back? And by it, she meant *him*. Eduardo.

But what had really changed in ten years? She couldn't go back to being the adoring teenager who'd had to wrestle her career from the hands of the man who claimed to love her and know what was best for her. He'd had their future all mapped out but hadn't been willing to alter those plans when his dreams had come crashing to the floor. He hadn't been willing to set aside his pride to follow her.

Maybe it had been for the best. She wasn't even leaving a trail of breadcrumbs to follow right now.

Her beloved abuela, who'd been her greatest support, had just died. Her manager-slash-best-friend-slash-husband was gone as well. Her mother no longer spoke to her. Angel's career was sinking out of sight. She was a lukewarm train wreck that would be lucky to get a guest appearance on a singing competition if she didn't get her act together soon.

She snatched her manuscript pad off the sofa and willed her muse out of retirement. But all that came to mind was the anger in Eduardo's eyes when he'd first spotted her yesterday. And his determination not to let her back into his life, even temporarily, as he'd walked out the door last night. She'd left too much devastation in her wake to restore even their friendship.

It wasn't his *friendship* she needed.

For the second time in less than twenty-four hours, Anna's heart raced as the lock on Eduardo's apartment door whirled open. Her hands shook, her knees shook… She was doing a good imitation of a willow tree in a hurricane.

For goodness' sake, she performed live in front of tens of thousands of people and didn't get this anxious. But there was so much more than her career riding on this next conversation.

In the long, lonely hours of the night, it had come to her: Eduardo was the only one she could trust with her dilemma. Everyone else she'd known pre-Angel had sold their stories about her to the media. Only Eduardo had kept silent. She could trust him. But whether he'd agree to her request was an entirely different matter. Her one hope that she wasn't about to go down in flames was that his body still reacted to hers.

And heaven knew, she wasn't immune to him. He was still the personification of temptation. In the past, he'd always been the one to stop before things went too far. Could she overcome that monumental self-control now?

One thing she had learned in the past decade was that people were more likely to do what you wanted if they saw the benefit to themselves. Was there any way she could spin her request so it sounded like a win for him?

She unfurled herself from where she sat on the sofa. Sleep had never been on the agenda. And she knew instinctively that Eduardo would try to slip in and out again without seeing her. So she'd stationed herself in the living room and waited. This was the only chance she was going to get. She had to seize it.

Damn the man. Did he have to look so utterly impeccable and gorgeous? It was barely six in the morning. He clearly hadn't spent the night in discomfort on a friend's too-short and lumpy sofa.

Had he stayed with some woman? Bile rose in her throat, and she reached for the glass of water she'd left on the coffee table.

He halted the second he saw her.

She cleared her throat before she could speak. "I'll go as soon as—"

"Your grandmother's funeral is tomorrow, isn't it?"

He had done his homework. The obituary hadn't given the time or location of the memorial service, as she'd wanted to keep it private. There were only a dozen people she knew her abuela would want there, and she'd contacted them personally. "Yes. At St. Felicitas at two o'clock. Do you want to attend?"

He dropped his phone and keys on the sideboard before stepping farther into the room. But he maintained his distance from her.

"And how long after the service will you be staying in Argentina?"

"I haven't booked my return flight. I have some … unfinished business I'd like to wrap up. Maybe a couple of days. A week at most."

He glanced at her, but his gaze skittered away just as quick. Maybe she wasn't playing fair, wearing one of his shirts. And only his shirt. But she was desperate.

"Then you might as well stay here. My friends are away in France. I can crash at their place. I'll just pack a few things." He moved towards his bedroom.

She followed.

"I don't mean to kick you out of your home. I can get another hotel room."

"I checked. Everything decent is booked solid. And I'd rather not have to go out in the middle of the night and rescue you again. I trust my neighbors; they're not going to set the building on fire."

"You weren't even in bed when I called you." She'd checked his room after he'd left last night. His bed had still been made up. Curiosity had always been her greatest weakness. "Had you just got in from a date?"

"No."

She just managed to stop herself from fist-pumping the air. "Why can't you stay here? The place is big enough. I promise to stay out of your way." Damn, she was sounding desperate even to her own ears.

He grabbed a bag from his closet and haphazardly threw items inside. If she didn't get his attention soon, he'd be gone and her future would be left in limbo. "My clothes smelled like smoke. I didn't think you'd mind, so I put them in your washer. I took this shirt out of the dirty laundry to wear in the meantime."

He paused. "You could have used a fresh one. Do you really think that I'd worry about you creating one more item for my housekeeper to clean?"

The one in the basket still smelled of him. Being surrounded by his scent was the only thing that had kept her from finishing off the whisky last night.

"Are you still a lawyer?" she asked.

He moved into the adjoining bathroom. "My license is current. But I'm not practicing anymore. If you need legal advice, I can recommend someone."

"I want you."

He tossed a shaving kit in the bag on his bed and then put his hands on his hips. "I just told you, I'm not practicing."

"Yes. But if I hired you, what I have to tell you would be in confidence, and you wouldn't be able to divulge it to anyone."

His eyes narrowed. "I'm a lawyer. Not a priest. Try the building down the road."

"It's not a confession. Well, it is, sort of. But a cleric can't help me. Only you can."

He moved back into his walk-in closet and called over his shoulder, "For the third time, I'm not practicing.

As soon as I finish helping Raul with his custody case, I'll let my license lapse. I'm a property developer now."

"If you're making an exception for Raul, surely you can make one for me too," she said when he reentered the bedroom. She ran her finger along the open neckline of the shirt she wore.

His fingers tightened on the ties he'd just taken from the wardrobe. "Raul is a friend."

Direct hit. Well, they didn't have to be friends for what she needed. "Please, Eduardo." She called up all her performance experience. Men like Eduardo didn't want desperate women. She tried again, injecting as much sultry temptress into her voice as she could. "I want you."

He closed his eyes for a moment. When he opened them again, he looked anywhere but at her. "I'm no longer a lawyer, Anna. And I definitely can't be *your* lawyer. We have history. Painful history. I couldn't offer you objective legal advice even if I wanted to."

She hauled in a deep breath. "I don't need advice. I need your body."

***

Every muscle in Eduardo reacted separately to Anna's statement. His cock swelled. His arms tensed, ready to sweep his suitcase to the floor and reclaim his shirt from her. His brain, however—which thankfully had control for now—froze.

Opening the door to find Anna waiting, wearing one of his shirts, had been like having a thousand hot needles pierce his eyeballs. It was everything he'd once dreamed of but now couldn't have. If she'd stayed all those years ago, if she hadn't ripped out his heart and trampled his soul, this is what he could have looked forward to every day. Now, it was just cruel to flaunt lost dreams in his face. Especially after he'd rescued her. Twice.

"Explain." The word came out harsh.

"Are we covered under lawyer-client confidentiality?" Her voice wavered, but her gaze remained firm.

"For God's sake, Anna—"

"Are we covered?"

"Yes, dammit!"

She nibbled her bottom lip, further tilting his see-sawing reactions towards lust. But even if she wanted him, it was only temporary. And if—no, when—she left, it would hurt all over again. Who was he kidding? It never stopped hurting. That had to end now.

He needed to ignore her plea. Pack his bag and head to Tiago's until he was sure she was out of the country. He owed her nothing. Even letting her stay here was more than she deserved. But somehow, he couldn't bring himself to ask her to leave or even take her up on her offer to go to another hotel. Maybe he was a masochist, enjoying the pain she inflicted on him. Maybe he enjoyed knowing she was in his space, touching his things, even if he couldn't, shouldn't, wouldn't touch her.

"I need help. Your help." Her words were barely above a whisper, but when she raised her eyes to his, all he saw was determination.

He crossed his arms to stop from reaching for her. "What kind of help?"

She glanced around. "Can we talk in the sitting room?"

"You're trying my patience, Anna. I've not slept or eaten or—"

She walked out of the bedroom! He was tempted to stay where he was and keep packing. But, like a lovesick puppy, he followed. He really should seek help for his Anna enchantment. Maybe he should be the one to visit the priest. Did they still do exorcisms?

"First, I need to tell you about my marriage," she began as he joined her in the lounge.

He held his hands before him. No way. No how. Not ever. "I don't want to hear it." What kind of sadist was she? She had to know he'd never want to discuss her relationship with her sixty-five-year-old husband.

"I know what you're thinking. It wasn't like that. Simon was everything wonderful and nice."

"I'm happy for you." Add some soda to his bitter words and he'd have an aperitif.

She poured him a glass of whisky and pointed at the sofa. "Sit and listen."

He placed the offering on the coffee table and stayed standing. He would not bow to her every command. "I'm not sure how your relationships with your other lawyers work, but this is not how I take instruction from my clients. If I still had clients. Which I don't. Because I am no longer practicing."

She shot him an exasperated look then began to pace the room. "Simon had three children by his first and second wives. They are each and every one of them parasites."

And all are older than you.

She glared at him as though she'd read his thought. As much as he wanted to disavow any knowledge of her life in LA, her marriage to her much, much older manager had made headlines for weeks in both gossip magazines and the legitimate press. It'd been impossible to avoid.

"And Simon left the bulk of his estate to you with only minimal bequests to his children," he said. "I can't help you. Even if I practiced estate law, this whole drama is playing out in the United States. I can't represent you there."

"I know. I have a team of lawyers already countering their lawsuits claiming I trapped Simon into marriage and unduly influenced him regarding the distribution of his assets. His children are trying to have the will dismissed."

"Then what do you want me for?"

She wrung her hands, and he felt the twist in his chest.

"My marriage was based on friendship and mutual need. I have my own money and have never needed, or wanted, his. Simon trusted me to ensure that his vision for the future succeeded. His wealth is to be used to further his dreams, not the whims of his freeloading children."

Eduardo nodded. He still couldn't see where he was involved.

She turned away and stared out the window. "My

stepchildren will seize every avenue to discredit my relationship with their father. If they find out my secret, not only will it give them the firepower they need, but it will also bring scandal and gossip to my life and Simon's legacy."

"What's your secret?"

She moved to stand straight in front of him. Her warm scent of vanilla and cinnamon enveloped him. Her blue eyes stared into his, searching, seeking. For what, he didn't know. But she must have found it.

"I'm still a virgin."

He blinked. What the hell? She was an international singing sensation, not a nun. She'd been living in LA for almost ten years. *Mierda*, she'd been married for three. How was this even possible? Because if there was one thing Anna did not lack, it was passion. Or sexiness, for that matter. He'd been in a near-constant state of arousal since walking through the door twenty minutes ago.

Hold on. Hadn't she said she needed his body? He reached around her and grabbed the whisky off the table, slinging it down his throat as though the liquid would illuminate the path to enlightenment.

Instead, it brought the unwelcome realization that Anna had waited for him.

He hadn't done the same.

A hesitant smile played around her lips. "Are you going to say something?"

The whisky made his voice husky. "Are you asking me to take your virginity?"

"Yes."

"Why? And why me? Seems you'd have a lot of

men to choose from."

She moved away, and he drew in a deep breath of Anna-free air. It didn't help.

"I want to have relationships. Normal relationships that involve physical intimacy. But I can't trust anyone with my secret. If word got out that Simon and I never consummated our marriage…"

"Anna, if you're going to be intimate with a man, you need to be able to trust him. If you can't trust, you shouldn't be climbing into bed with him." He ruthlessly shut down the image of Anna naked in another man's arms.

"Why risk it when I know I can trust you? Plus, we have lawyer-client privilege."

"I can't sleep with a client. It's unethical. I could be disbarred."

She sauntered over to him, and he steeled himself. She didn't disappoint. Resting one hand over his chest before sliding it up and around his neck, her fingers burrowing into the short hair at his nape, urging his head down towards hers. Her other hand slid around his waist, pulling herself flush against him. Every single cell in his body reacted as if he'd never been with a woman before. Well, not a woman like Anna, anyway.

"But we've already established that your days as a lawyer are at an end. What do you say, Edio?" Dammit, she didn't play fair. She caressed his name, whispered it full of longing and passion. "Will you take me to bed? Be my first lover?"

Once, he'd wanted to be her first. And her last. Her only.

He pulled away before she lured him deeper under her spell—before he lost what little remained of his heart and his pride. She'd left him. Now she wanted to use him.

"I'll think about it," he said.

Her eyes widened at his reply but then narrowed again. "You'll *think* about it? What's to think about? You wanted me in the past." She stared pointedly at his groin. "You want me now. This would be a way to close the chapter of us. Give it a good ending."

Or it could ruin the rest of his story. "Unlike you, I make rational, well-thought-out decisions. I don't sell my soul for the promise of fame and fortune."

She turned away, but not before he saw a flash of hurt in her eyes. Dammit, he would not feel like a bastard for stating the obvious. She'd rescind her request now, and he'd be spared the agony of imagining the two of them together at last.

She turned back to him, however, and he saw determination in her face. "Think fast, then," she said. "You've got two days to give me your answer."

No matter how much he still desired her, he would not be manipulated.

But Dios, the temptation…

Chapter Four

Anna knew the minute Eduardo arrived at her grandmother's funeral. A sense of calm, of rightness, of peace flowed through her despite the anguish of burying the woman who had loved her unconditionally.

There were only a dozen or so mourners in the church. After the debacle at the community center and the terror of the hotel fire, her staff had 'leaked' photos of her in Sweden. They'd been taken during her last visit there but had not been released at the time. Now her fans and the international media thought she was on the opposite side of the world.

Anna forced her brain to concentrate on the priest's words as he enumerated the many blessings of life in heaven awaiting the pious like Marta Marquez. Anna's thoughts were earthly. A day later and she was still trying to assimilate Eduardo's reply to her request. He'd raced to his room, grabbed his half-packed bag, and shot out the door before she'd even pulled in a full breath.

She'd always thought that when she finally offered herself to a man, she'd be on her back before the words had escaped her lips. Trust Eduardo to be different. For a second, she'd thought maybe he didn't want her. But his body didn't lie, even if his mouth did.

She glanced across the aisle to see if he had joined Raul in the pew a few rows back. Eduardo's driver had arrived at the apartment just as she'd been about to call a taxi. He'd brought his adorable little boy with him, both of them wearing black suits, explaining that if anyone were watching for her, arriving with a man and child would hopefully put them off the scent. For her part, she was dressed in a long-sleeved black dress and had her hair bundled under a wide-brimmed hat with a full veil. Not to mention the oversized sunglasses hiding her unusual eyes. She barely recognized herself.

A sad smile lifted her lips. Abuela would have appreciated the drama of her outfit. She'd always been a fashionable lady, even if she'd had the money to buy nice clothes only after Anna had ripped out her heart and sold her soul to the music industry.

The priest finally finished, and it was time for her to sing her grandmother's favorite hymn. Her gaze skimmed over the small congregation. Her grandmother's closest friends were all here. Anna's mother, Abuela's only child, wasn't. Would Anna's funeral be equally devoid of family, the church filled with people who cared only for what she had done for them?

As she began the first line of 'On Eagle's Wings,' her gaze met Eduardo's. Although the words were about the strength the Lord gave, he was the one she thought of. He was the one who'd inspired her, believed in her, lifted her up when she was down—loved her. Ironically, it had been that love, and the resulting courage and confidence, that had given her the strength to fulfill her dreams.

Eduardo looked away. Anna sang the rest of the hymn with her eyes on her abuela's photo. The last note echoed in the church like a spirit delaying departure.

The first tear broke the dam, and the priest had to help her back to her seat. Her one glance upward confirmed what her heart already knew. Eduardo was gone. She heard nothing of the rest of the mass. She only knew it had ended when she was surrounded by a cluster of her grandmother's friends, all crying as much as she was.

Abuela's passing had been expected. She'd lived three times longer than the doctors had predicted when she'd first been diagnosed with cancer. Mostly, Anna suspected, because Abuela loved to prove people wrong.

Now her grandmother was free of pain, but it seemed to have transferred to her granddaughter instead. Anna pulled in an unsteady breath at the same time a large, warm hand settled on the center of her back. Had the touch been accompanied by tingles, she would know it was Eduardo.

She turned slightly and smiled as best she could at Raul. "I will be waiting by the door when you are ready to leave," he said quietly.

"Where's Timo?" She looked around but couldn't see the little boy.

"Señor Forenza took him outside. He was restless."

Who was restless, Eduardo or Timo? Before she could ask, her grandmother's closest friend put a hand on Anna's arm.

"Take your time," Raul said before slipping away.

"She loved you very much and was so proud of what you achieved," Eva Vasquez said. "Although she didn't like your husband. She always hoped you'd get back together with that Eduardo. Was that who you were looking at during the hymn? Now he is a man worthy of you."

Ah, the candor of the aged. You could always rely on them to tell it like it was. Anna ignored the comment. It wasn't anything her grandma hadn't told her personally. Numerous times.

Anna attempted a smile. "I wish I had been here to hold her hand in the end."

The grip on her arm tightened. "Don't torture yourself with what can't be changed. Marta wouldn't have known if you were there or not. She was sedated beyond comprehension in the last ten days."

"At least she wasn't in pain." Anna said the words, although they gave no comfort. She should have made the time, should have canceled her last appearance and missed the court date to be at her grandmother's bedside.

"All she ever wanted was for you to be happy, Anna. It's what we all want." Eva gestured at the other women arranged around her like a geriatric intervention. "Either start again, with a young man this time, or fix what must be mended from the past. But don't put your singing before love. You're a smart girl. Don't make the same mistake again." A pat on the cheek accompanied these last pearls of wisdom.

If Anna's ego ever inflated, she knew where to come to get a grip on reality. Her gaze swept to the back of the church, but Eduardo was truly gone. Only Raul stood there, looking like the church bouncer.

Sitting alone in Eduardo's apartment the night before, she'd let herself dream that he'd stride back through the door and, without words, sweep her into his arms, carry her tenderly to his room, and make love to her all afternoon and well into the evening. Then, when they were both too satiated to move, he'd look into her eyes and tell her that he'd never stopped loving her and he would never let her go.

Then what? He'd give up everything and follow her around the world while she resuscitated her singing career and set up her late husband's legacy? Or would he demand that she return to Argentina and become the dutiful wife who looked good on his arm while he schmoozed planning committees and investors?

No matter what happened in the next two days, they had no future.

The old ladies were right. It was time to start over. Now. Before she lost her nerve.

She'd tell Eduardo the offer was off the table—or, more literally, off the bed. New plan: head back to LA, write a hit song about the folly of trying to resurrect a dead love, and live happily ever after in her ivory mansion in the sky.

Job done.

***

Eduardo stood in the shade cast by one of the street trees, idly rubbing Timo's back. The little boy had his thumb in his mouth, his face tucked against Eduardo's neck, almost asleep. It was during moments like this that Eduardo was bombarded with the what-might-have-beens. If Anna had stayed, would they have a little boy now? Eduardo's throat thickened. Timo wasn't even his son, and still love swelled within him whenever he held the child.

From the moment he'd first encountered the little boy—terrified, clinging to Raul while his mother screamed in the courthouse hallway—he'd felt a kinship with the toddler. He didn't regret extending a legal career he'd intended to give up when it meant that Timo went to sleep each night safe, knowing he was loved and not a pawn in a battle between embittered adults.

The resultant friendship with Raul had been another bonus. A common background made it easy for them to understand each other. Tiago, Eduardo's other close friend, had had his share of issues—but money had never been one of them. Raul understood Eduardo's drive, his need to build his own empire, be his own man. Relying on others was a recipe for disaster. They left. Anna was proof of that. If he'd followed her to LA all those years ago, eventually she'd have tired of him. And then he'd have had nothing. At least now he had something. Even if it was just the opportunity to lull someone else's child to sleep.

But, Dios, every time he saw her, he was struck with thoughts of what could have been. Taking Timo outside was the only excuse he'd been able to come up with to flee the service.

To flee Anna.

He shouldn't have come. It had been a last-minute decision.

On the way to St. Felicitas church, he'd reasoned that he was going to pay his final respects to Marta Marquez. But his thoughts had only been about Anna. In his heart, he knew he should keep his distance from her. She could find some other man to be her first. Or hell, even a sex toy could probably do the job she wanted. After the funeral, he'd tell her no.

But hearing her sing in person had been too intimate, even with a dozen other people present, including a priest. Every perfectly pitched note had been a laser, slicing away the time between then and now.

He had a fairly iffy relationship with God. But just in case He did exist, surely it was flirting with disaster to be thinking of sex in a church.

He knew, though, in the depths of his soul, that making love to Anna even once would affect him forever. Seeing her again... All the times he'd told himself he was over her, he'd been lying. He wasn't going to relive a painful parting for one night with his ex.

Even outside, Anna's voice floated on the breeze through the partially open church door. He'd never doubted she'd be a star. Selfishly, though, he hadn't wanted to share her with the world. At least not at eighteen. He'd encouraged her to wait until she turned twenty-one before taking her singing professional. In this, at least, her grandmother had been his ally.

They'd had it all worked out. By the time she was out of her teens, he'd be a professional rugby player, most likely playing for one of the wealthy European clubs. He'd be making his own fortune and able to support the launch of her career. Then together they'd conquer the world.

His injury had obliterated that path. She'd wait, he'd told himself while the doctor explained the likely outcome of the surgery—the end of his professional rugby playing days. Anna would hold his hand and help him recover. Then they'd make a new plan.

While he'd been under the knife, she'd come up with her own strategy. She'd cashed in on the song she'd written about the death of his dreams. Then she'd pursued her dreams, leaving him in agony in a hospital bed thousands of kilometers away.

Maybe if he'd helped her get some local singing gigs, she'd have stuck around. Maybe if she'd started her career in BA, she wouldn't have had to fly so far away. What if, what if. How many nights had he tortured himself with these thoughts?

It all boiled down to this one reality: Anna had the option of him or fame. She'd chosen fame.

Like his grandmother always said, he'd never be anyone's first choice.

Timo mumbled something, and Eduardo lightened the pressure of his hand on the child's back. He'd almost squished the poor boy. *Enough.* No more thoughts of Anna. It had happened. They were different people now. They had to find a way to close the door on the past and move on.

A few mourners began to filter out of the church. He told himself not to look, but his eyes dismissed each person until they lighted on Anna. Not even the severity of her all-black attire could diminish the light that seemed to emanate only from her.

As if sensing his gaze, she raised her head and caught him staring. She excused herself from the person she was talking to and made her way over to him.

She nodded at little Timo. "Suits you," she said, her voice husky. She'd been crying. His heart lurched, and he hugged the boy a little tighter, even though Raul was now next to him, arms out, ready to take his son.

"What does?"

"Fatherhood. How come you never married and had children of your own?"

"You have to ask that?"

She had the sense to glance down at the ground. But not before he'd seen the hurt in her eyes. Damn, he needed to stop giving away how much he was still affected by her betrayal.

And they both needed to stop pretending they could have any kind of relationship now. Some things were meant to be a lesson and not a happily-ever-after.

"Boss, are you coming back to the apartment with us?" Raul's question shattered the silence.

Being in a confined space with Anna was more than he was capable of withstanding at the moment. She may be his not-all-love-lasted lesson, but clearly, he hadn't learned all the nuances yet. He still wanted her. Fiercely.

"No. I've got Tiago's SUV. I'm heading back to the office anyway."

Raul nodded. "*Señorita* Marquez, I will get Timo settled in his safety seat. We can go whenever you're ready. The car is just across the street."

She gave Raul a watery smile, but no words escaped her lips.

Eduardo transferred the now-sleeping boy to his father's arms. Raul already had the keys in hand and clicked the unlock button.

Kaboom!

The lightning Eduardo had feared earlier in church turned the daylight blinding. The shock wave hit them next, followed swiftly by chunks of metal and glass, and a deafening roar.

He dived for Anna, knocking her to the ground as much as the blast had done. He covered her with his body, bearing the brunt of the debris that rained down on them for what seemed like an eternity.

Screams filled the air. Eduardo raised his head enough to see that Raul had similarly sheltered Timo. The fronds of the palm tree that had stood in the church's courtyard were blown off and now partially covered their bodies, providing flimsy protection against the flying missiles.

Car and building alarms blared. Within seconds, the sirens of emergency services vehicles joined the cacophony.

"Are you hurt?" he asked Anna.

At least his rugby career had taught him how to land without doing too much injury. Stabs of pain echoed through his collarbone, but he'd deal with that discomfort later.

It took her a second to reply, long enough for him to start an inventory of her limbs. "I'm okay. What happened?"

"Stay down while I check."

"But—" She started to sit up.

"Just this once, Anna, listen to me."

She lay back down but began to inch her way towards Raul and Timo. The big man was rising as well, running his hands over his son to search for injuries. The little boy was whimpering, although it appeared to be more from fright than pain.

Eduardo scanned the courtyard. Several others had been thrown to the ground by the blast, but there didn't appear to be any serious injuries; all body parts were still attached at least. Most of the funeral's attendees had stayed at the far side of the building. If anyone had been closer... Thankfully, the chest-high stone walls around the churchyard had provided some protection.

What remained of his vehicle was now on fire. All the windows of the building beside it were shattered. Glass was strewn about the sidewalk and roadway.

Raul crouched next to Eduardo, a sobbing Timo in his arms. "Take Timo and Señorita Marquez back into the church," Raul said. Every vestige of civilization had disappeared from his face. Here was a man ready to rip apart the world to find the person responsible for endangering his son.

"I—"

"Señor Forenza, this is one of the reasons you hired me. I will make sure it's safe and then get you all out of here. Where is Señor Alvarez's SUV?"

"It's parked on Azara by Suarez. I paid a boy to watch it." Eduardo handed over the keys as Raul transferred Timo into his arms.

"I'll get it." He clenched the keys. "If something happens to me, will you look after Timo? Don't let that bitch get him."

Eduardo nodded, and Raul darted around the debris that was strewn about the courtyard. For a big man, he moved quickly.

The priest had emerged from the church and was ushering people inside. Anna held her arms out for Timo as Eduardo moved them towards the solid stone building. It would be easier to protect them if he had his arms free, so he let her take the small child.

The stained-glass windows on one side of the church had been blown in. Colored shards littered the pews and aisle, glittering in the unfiltered sunlight. Despite the destruction, it was still beautiful.

The shaken cleric rushed over to them. "Are you okay?" he asked.

"We're uninjured," Eduardo answered. "How are the others?"

"A few cuts and more than a few bruises, I suspect. *Señora* Vasquez may have re-injured her hip. But everyone is, *gracias a Dios*, alive."

Eduardo nodded. He could now turn his attention to the cause of the blast. Or, more importantly, to its intended victim or victims. His gaze caught Anna's. Her whole body was shaking. He wrapped both arms around her and Timo. This was the third incident involving her. It was hard to believe they weren't somehow connected. But there was no denying he'd made a few enemies himself.

Now, however, wasn't the time to compile a list. They had to get to safety.

"Is there a back way out of here?" he asked.

"Yes, through the priest's door at the side of the chancel. But shouldn't you stay to speak with the police?"

He handed the man one of his business cards. "They can call me for a statement. But I saw nothing. And please"—he leveled his sternest stare, usually reserved for an uncooperative court witness—"keep the name *Angel* from slipping past your lips. If her being here remains a secret, I will personally pay to have the church's windows replaced."

"I will pray for you all," the priest said before directing them through several back corridors to a small room with a door to the exterior. He undid the six locks while Eduardo called Raul to let him know the pickup point.

Minutes later, with a squeal of the tires, they were speeding away from the church and the devastation.

"Where to, boss?" Raul asked.

"The airport. We're all getting the hell out of town while we figure out who is after which one of us."

Anna shot him a confused look. But instead of demanding an explanation, she said, "I have to pick up something from your apartment."

Dios, did she not understand the danger she was in? "We can't risk it. If someone is after us, my apartment will be the first place they'll look."

"Please, Eduardo. It's vitally important to me." A tear threatened at the corner of her right eye. He'd noticed a few fall since they'd been in the car. It wasn't one of her better days. Actually, her whole week had been pretty upsetting. And it was only Wednesday.

Raul caught his gaze in the rearview mirror, his eyes full of compassion. "Señorita Miranda's pet is also there." He said it as though Eduardo would more likely be persuaded to care for a cat rather than cave to the whims of a woman who seemed to cause chaos wherever she went.

"My housekeeper—"

"Please, Eduardo," Anna repeated. "It will only take me a second to grab it."

Mierda. Didn't they know he was trying to keep everyone safe? "All right. But I will get what you want. You're to stay in the car with Raul." If they were headed towards an ambush, at least some of them could escape.

"Thank you." Her voice broke, and the tears began in earnest.

If Timo weren't between them, he'd take her in his arms.

And then they'd both be lost.

Chapter Five

Anna flung her hat on the bed and kicked off her shoes with such force one bounced off the wall. Eduardo had insisted she stay 'in disguise' until she was inside the house. Her guitar, the item she'd insisted on bringing with her, received gentler treatment. She rested it in its case against the dresser, in sight of the bed.

How long until the shakes from the explosion left her hands? Her ears still rang with the sound. Right now, she didn't care if the hearing loss was a career killer. She was too happy to still be alive and whole.

If Eduardo hadn't dived on her, she'd have topped Carrie Underwood in the facial injury charts. His suit had been shredded, and she'd noticed the bloodstains on his shirt when he'd removed his jacket. But he'd refused her offer to help bandage his injuries. Was his terse tone due to pain or her continued presence in his life?

Not that he'd given her any other option. He'd taken over again—made decisions without her input. And she'd slipped back into the besotted girlfriend role. Grief, exhaustion, feeling adrift … they had all conspired to turn her into a weak-kneed woman who let a man run her life. Good thing her mother wasn't speaking to her, or Valentina would have a few choice words for Anna's damsel-in-distress impersonation.

Tomorrow she'd wrest back control. But just for now, she was grateful someone had a plan. Because she had no clue what to do. Hopefully, a good night's sleep would cure that. Whether she'd get it or not was anyone's guess.

At least the room wouldn't be to blame. Bright and airy, decorated in cream tones, with a cement balcony overlooking the vineyards and mountains beyond, it was the essence of comfortable. The king-sized sleigh bed was covered in a fluffy duvet, with a navy blue blanket draped across the bottom for added warmth. The whole place was amazing. As far as safe houses went, this one erred on the side of magnificent.

Maybe a soak in the claw-foot tub in the adjoining bathroom would help her relax. Eduardo had spent the drive to the airport making calls and arrangements on his cell phone while keeping everything very mysterious. It wasn't until the Andes came into view through the tiny window of the private jet that she realized where they were heading.

Mendoza. Back to where it all fell apart. This was where Eduardo had been playing when he was injured. This was where he'd stayed, finished his degree, and made friends, including the owner of this stunning mansion set among the vineyards.

Here, she and Eduardo could finally talk, make peace with each other. Here, she could start over.

If only someone wasn't trying to kill her.

So much for her revised plan to head back to LA and forget Eduardo. They were stuck together for at least a few more days. Her glance strayed once more to the large, inviting bed. Should she still rescind her offer? Or wait for him to decide?

Dammit, she was back to square one.

"Señorita?" She turned to find a young woman standing in the open doorway. The maid's mouth dropped open.

Anna pasted on a weary smile. Angel, with her sweetness and light, who always made time for her fans, refused to make an appearance. "Yes?"

"Señor Forenza asked me to bring you some clothes. They belong to Señora Alvarez, but she won't mind if you wear them. Would you like me to put them away for you?"

"No, I can do that. Thank you."

The young woman placed the items on the bed then backed towards the door. "He also asked me to tell you that he is down on the terrace if you'd like to join him."

At least she wasn't being confined to her room. "Please let him know that I'll just have a wash and be down shortly."

The woman bobbed a curtsy—people still did that?—then shut the door behind her.

Anna selected a bohemian skirt and caftan top from the pile of clothes on the bed. These items, among the predominantly fitted dresses, offered comfort. She started to wind her hair into a chignon but at the last minute decided to pull it into a high ponytail instead.

She relegated the relaxing bath until before bed and headed downstairs. From there, hopefully, she'd be able to find the terrace and Eduardo. The house was built in a U-shape around a central courtyard, but there seemed to be hallways and doors everywhere. Maybe there was a map of the house she could use to find her way.

In the end, she didn't need assistance. She heard him before she saw him. His deep, authoritative voice drew her like a dancer to music.

He'd changed out of his shredded suit and now wore a pair of dark jeans and a loose button-up shirt a few sizes too big. He was, of course, on his phone, but as soon as he caught sight of her, he ended the call with an "I've got to go. I'll speak with you later. Text me when you have any information."

She stepped onto the tiled terrace; the warmth of the sun-warmed flooring banished some of the chill from her bare feet. "Who were you talking to?"

Without asking, he handed her a drink. She didn't even inquire what was in the tall glass with moisture condensing on the outside. A sip revealed a tangy lemonade with a kicker of vodka.

"A friend on the police force."

"And?"

"Let me worry about it. You just relax."

Forget tomorrow. She was taking the reins back now, with or without a plan.

She put the drink down on the glass table and went toe-to-toe with him. It wasn't as intimidating a position as she'd hoped because she still had to stretch her neck to meet his gaze. And take a second breath because his nearness stole the first from her lungs. Still, she wasn't going to stand in the wings while her life was on the line.

"I'm not a child, Eduardo. This involves me. I have a right to know what's happening and who's behind these incidents."

He ran a shaky hand through his hair and retreated a step. "They're still investigating the bombing. As for the fire, they found accelerant in the hotel suite, so it was definitely arson. But they don't have a list of suspects yet, and therefore they don't know whether flushing you out of your room was the motive or if someone had a grudge against the hotel. They've re-interviewed the kid who threw the firecracker into the community center. He said he was paid to do it, but he couldn't provide a reliable description of the person who had hired him."

She picked up her glass and took a long drink. To keep her eyes from devouring Eduardo, she wandered over to an arrangement of flowers tumbling from a cement urn. "I never imagined that Simon's children would go to these lengths. Suing me is one thing. Trying to kill me…"

"You're assuming that you are the target," he said.

Her gaze snapped back to him. "Of course I'm the target. All three incidents involve me."

"The first involved me too. And I had more to lose than you from the disruption of the meeting. The planners have put the application on hold. It's costing me money each day we're delayed."

"But the fire—"

"You were booked into the hotel using my last name. Why, by the way?"

She shrugged, feigning nonchalance. Reminder for next time: never make a hotel reservation after a third lemon drop martini. "I always book into hotels with fake names. I didn't bring security with me so I decided to use a common Argentine name to put off any followers. Yours was the first one that came to mind." *And let's not analyze that.*

"Forenza's not that common."

"Well, last time I used Eva Perón, and that was worse."

He smiled, but there was still disbelief in his eyes. "Someone with your talents should have more imagination. And people to reserve hotels for you."

"Yeah. Sometimes I like to do things for myself, just to prove I still can."

He raised one eyebrow but only asked, "And the *Mrs.*? Why claim to be my wife?"

"I wasn't claiming to be your wife." Although she could see how he'd think that. "I was just…" There was no way to end that sentence without further incriminating herself. Caught up in nostalgia and vodka, she'd used a name that would have been hers if she'd made a different choice all those years ago.

He stared into her eyes for a few more seconds, and she could almost see the battle going on. Should he pursue this line of questioning, one that would undoubtedly lead to an agonizing rehash of the past? Or stick with the present issue? Thankfully, he chose the latter. "It doesn't matter what name you used. I was seen dropping you off. Thankfully, the paparazzi who took the photo didn't get a clean look at you, but it was still up on social media sites that I was at the hotel with a woman. And it was my car that was blown up at the church."

Someone could be after Eduardo? *Mierda*, that did

not make her feel better.

"Who would want you dead?"

His laugh held no humor. "More people than you can imagine. But off the top of my head, Miranda's other uncle. I was instrumental in making sure that Tiago got custody of his niece, and as a result, he kept control of his company, which allowed me to become partner."

"Seems a little extreme."

"You don't know Spencer Suarez. He's insane. And he's used explosives before. He blew out the windows of the building across from Tiago's to trigger Vivi's PTSD." Anna had no idea who these people were, but now wasn't the time to get distracted.

"And this Spencer Suarez is still in Buenos Aires?"

"Well, currently, he's in prison somewhere in Argentina. But that wouldn't stop him from getting someone on the outside to do his dirty work. He's very resourceful."

She swallowed that information with the rest of her drink. Her knees decided to confirm her earlier self-assessment and gave way. Thankfully, there was a sofa right behind her.

"I could also be the target." Raul's aggressive tone matched his clenched fists as he strode onto the terrace. "I caught sight of one of my old *acquaintances* when I parked the car this afternoon. He'd have had the skills and necessary equipment to blow the vehicle."

Eduardo became alert, like a dog hearing the fridge door open. "Why didn't you say something earlier?"

Raul looked down for a moment then raised his eyes to Eduardo's face and straightened his shoulders.

"Because Timo was present. I'd rather he didn't learn just yet that his father was once a drug dealer and gang enforcer."

Eduardo nodded as though this wasn't news to him. "Where is Timo now?"

"With the cook." Raul's face softened again. "They're baking a cake. She promised him he could decorate it and we'd have it for dessert."

Eduardo ran his hand again through his hair while he paced the terrace. "So any of the three of us could have been the target of the bombing."

Anna's first instinct was to soothe the anxiety on his face. She didn't have the right. A nervous giggle escaped her. "Wow, we're some badass group," she said.

Both men turned and looked at her as though she were crazy. Finally, a smile tugged at Eduardo's sensual lips. "I guess we are."

Raul's face still looked like thunder. "Boss, I'm sorry I put you and Señorita Marquez in danger. If you can look after Timo for a couple of days, I'll go back to BA and sort this all out."

"No." Eduardo's harsh reply made Anna jump.

Raul seemed unfazed. "Okay, I'll take Timo with me. I'm sure I can find someone to watch him."

"That's not what I meant, and you know it. You have to stay here. We all have to stay here. It's time to let law enforcement figure this out." Raul looked unconvinced, but Eduardo pressed on. "Besides, if whoever is behind all these attempts follows us to Mendoza, I may need you to get Anna and Timo to safety."

"What if I left?" Anna asked. Again, both men raised their eyebrows. "I mean, what if I returned to America? I can rehire a security team, and my house is like a fortress. Simon was a bit paranoid." If anything happened to anyone because of her, the guilt would eat her alive.

Eduardo took the seat beside her. His hand covered hers where it plucked at the fringes of a throw pillow. "Until we know who's behind this, we all stay here. We're safe. I've hired an elite team of former special ops commandos to keep the place secure."

"Um, exactly what type of law have you been practicing?" Surely not every lawyer had mercenaries on speed dial. Then again, probably not many had a former drug dealer as a driver either.

"Tiago's half brother's half brother, Jacques, has connections. Complicated family, but very useful."

She nodded. Useful family was something she did not have. In fact, she had no one she could trust. Except the man sitting beside her.

Her life was in danger, but she was no longer terrified. Was it so wrong that she was secretly thrilled she wouldn't be saying goodbye to Eduardo anytime soon?

Perhaps it was time to reattempt a seduction.

***

Beside him, Anna laced her fingers with his. Her anxiety flowed through that tight grip. Dios, he could have lost her today. Which was ridiculous, because he'd lost her long ago.

She appeared impossibly young in her borrowed clothes. The olive green gypsy skirt brushed the floor; her bare toes peeped beneath the voluminous material when she walked. The loose, cream-colored top hinted at the curves beneath but kept them thankfully concealed. She'd removed her makeup. She was back to the Anna he'd known long ago. But this Anna was no longer his.

Raul's eyes focused on their entwined fingers before a small smile appeared. "I'd better go check on Timo. Knowing him, he's charmed the cook into letting him make dinner."

He should ask Raul to stay. Being alone with Anna was not a good idea. There was no telling what stupid declarations he'd make. Before he could form the words, however, his friend reentered the house.

He steeled himself to look at her. Her blue eyes were clouded, her teeth nibbling on her bottom lip. Ah, *mierda…*

He could be a brick wall tomorrow. He wrapped an arm around her, pulling her tightly against his side.

Offering her comfort was simply him being a decent guy. It wouldn't lead to more. A modicum of peace flowed through him. He needed it after a day where he'd been too close to the edge of sanity—too close to the edge of savagery. In the immediate aftermath of the explosion, he'd been willing, almost eager, to find the culprits and pound them into next week. He'd come to think of himself as suave and sophisticated. It'd taken only one blast to prove he was more like his impulsive father than he ever wanted to be.

He'd once thought that with Anna in his arms he could conquer the world. That same illusion flirted with his willpower now. But he was wiser. He hoped.

"How did you meet Raul?" She raised her face to his, and he saw determination in the depths of her eyes. A neutral topic of conversation would benefit them both.

"I met him in the courthouse. I'd just finished hammering out a temporary custody arrangement for Tiago's niece when there was a disruption in the hallway. Raul was standing there, clutching a terrified Timo while a woman screamed obscenities and pounded him with her fists. He could have easily flattened her with one swing." Eduardo's father would have done it without another thought. "I admired Raul's restraint."

"Was the woman Timo's mother? Raul told me that she'd abandoned them but was back now and suing for custody."

"Yes. She'd just walked out one day, no note, leaving a one-year-old Timo in his cot until Raul came home later that evening to a screaming child. Then about six months ago, she showed up on the arm of someone high up in the gang Raul used to associate with. He worries that if Timo spends time with his mother, eventually he'll end up in gang life. Not to mention his mother's volatile personality being a concern. I…"

"You don't want Timo to end up with an unstable woman if you can help it," she finished for him. He nodded. Anna was the only person who knew the sorry tale of his childhood and youth. He didn't talk about it with anyone. Not even Raul. It wasn't because he was embarrassed about where he'd come from. In fact, he was proud of what he'd accomplished with nothing but hard work. It simply didn't matter. He was no longer that person. But if he had his way, no other child would go through that either.

"Yes. Raul told me didn't have the money to pay me. He didn't even have employment, because no one wanted to hire an ex-con, especially one who had ties to one of BA's most notorious gangs. So I offered him a job."

"And a place to live?"

"That was a little later. Where they were living … it would have been too easy for Raul to fall back into his old habits. He had the strength to recognize his weakness, the lure of easy money when he was trying to rebuild his life for Timo's sake. They stayed at my place for a week while he found a new apartment. I was gone for most of the time anyway. They could have stayed longer, but Raul isn't keen on 'charity.' He wants to stand on his own two feet and provide for Timo honestly."

"He's doing an amazing job. Timo clearly loves him, and you. You're very sweet with the little boy as well."

Red flags waved furiously in his mind. They were not going there. Those dreams of a family with her were gone. Time to redirect the conversation.

"Tell me about your career. What is your favorite thing about being an international pop star?"

She shifted as though uncomfortable. He loosened his hold on her shoulder, but she only moved closer. "I wouldn't say I'm a star…"

He brushed a few strands of her hair away from her cheek. It was like the softest silk slipping though his fingers. "You're internationally known by one name. You're a star."

She shrugged, a faint blush staining her cheeks. "In my heart, I'm still just Anna Marquez. As for my career, I like writing songs the best. Well, usually. I've been struggling lately. I also enjoy performing. My least favorite things are marketing and probably recording—singing the same song over and over until the producer is happy. It's exhausting."

"And the travel?" They'd often spoken of the places they'd visit together. Another dream gone.

"It's not like I imagined," she said.

"Yeah, I've been on a few international business trips. I'm so exhausted after the meetings that I've no desire to visit the sites."

"With me, it's that I want to share the experience with someone who matters to me. Instead, it all turns into a big publicity event."

"I guess that's the price you pay for fame."

She pulled out of his arms and stood before him, her hands stretched out as though pleading her case. "I never wanted to be famous, you know. I just wanted to sing and make people happy and maybe make a bit of money so I wouldn't have to worry about becoming homeless."

His shrug was more stiff than relaxed. "And you didn't trust that I could provide that life for you."

"Dios, Eduardo. Do you think I didn't believe in you? I always knew you'd be a success—whether on the rugby field or in the world of business. You have the drive and the brains to do anything you want. When you got injured—"

"You left."

"No! I saw another way for us both to have what we always wanted. I had a recording contract, a very good one. I could have supported you while you figured out your next steps. You could have stayed in rugby, trained to go into coaching or management. You loved the sport; I wanted to help you keep doing that. You could have recovered in LA while I recorded my album…"

It was the same tune as the argument they'd had over the phone while he'd waited for his surgery, just with different words.

"You know that never would have worked. I can never be a man who lives off a woman. You'd have lost respect for me. Hell, I'd have lost respect for myself. Then you would have left me anyway." Ten years later, and the bitterness of her sudden departure still welled within him. The anger, the hopelessness, the feeling of unworthiness—all familiar acids dripping on his soul.

"Why? Because of your mother? I'm not her and never will be. I would never run off and abandon my husband and child."

He stood as well, needing to move. "It was a risk I couldn't take. The parallel between our romance and my parents' marriage was too close to ignore. My father had been training to be a millwright, but he gave it up to follow my mother in her career. Then when I was born, his family pressured my mother to quit modeling, saying that children needed stability, needed to go to bed in the same room each night. Without a trade, Papa found it difficult to get work. Mama hated staying at home, living with nothing. Neither of them had ever been any good at saving money. She grew restless and left. And because my father had basically lived through her, he had nothing to fill the void. He crawled into a bottle and never escaped until he died—with a glass in one hand, my mother's photo in the other."

"I… I didn't know. Why didn't you tell me?"

"Would it have made a difference?"

She sighed. "I don't know."

"A lot of it I didn't know myself until after Papa died and I went through his papers. Growing up, I knew my mother left, although I didn't know why. But my father continually told me I had to be my own man, to make my own way in life, not to rely on anyone. Even without knowing the whole story, I saw how things had turned out for him, and I didn't want to end up the same."

"You wouldn't have become him."

But hadn't he? He'd replaced dependence on alcohol with a business suit and lost himself in his career. When was the last time he'd had fun?

"I thought you'd come back," he said, barely recognizing his own voice. "I worked and worked so I'd have something to prove to you I was worthy, that I was more than a failed athlete."

"You were always worthy, Eduardo. You were everything to me. But that was also part of the problem. I had to have a life as well. If I hadn't taken that chance, I think eventually I would have resented you for denying me my dream."

Yeah, he could see that now. They'd been too focused on a perfect imaginary future to see that what they had then was worth fighting for. Unfortunately, he'd never been one to compromise, to deviate from a plan once formed.

Was he any different now? He still had plans; he'd mapped out his future. Anna wasn't part of it.

Was he repeating the same mistake again?

Chapter Six

They say hindsight is twenty-twenty, but Anna still felt that any decision she made back then would have ended in heartbreak.

Her mother had insisted that she sign the recording contract and leave immediately for LA. Valentina had been the one to upload to YouTube Anna's song about Eduardo losing his dream career. And once the representative from the record company had shown up, her mother had been so excited. They had a shot at getting out of Boca, at "living the life they deserved." For the first time in Anna's existence, her mother had been pleased with something her daughter had done.

So she'd caved to her mother's demand, hoping to finally make up for her birth. Anna had been the unwanted result of her mother's teenage indiscretion with a tourist who had promised to show her the world and instead left her knocked up at home.

As far as Anna could tell, the pregnancy test result was the last positive in Valentina Marquez's life. Nothing Anna did ever made her mother pleased that she'd had a daughter. Then a stranger had knocked at the door and offered Valentina a hundred grand up front to relocate to America and turn the child she'd never wanted into the world's darling.

Eduardo's stubborn refusal to follow her had sealed their fate.

The high of finally achieving maternal approval had lasted two years. Then the cracks started to show. More and more of Valentina's demands had been about pleasing herself rather than advancing Anna's career. Finally, the day after Anna turned twenty-one, she appointed Simon as her music manager and her mother as her "lifestyle" manager. That had appeased Valentina a little. But soon even that wasn't enough.

With Eduardo no longer in the picture, Anna plowed all her energy, all her passion, into her songs and performances. She achieved success beyond her imagination. Enough to pay her mother a hefty monthly sum to keep out of her life.

But now, standing before her former boyfriend, she wished that somewhere along the line she'd done things differently. She had so many designer clothes, shoes, and handbags she'd never have to repeat an outfit for years. Three supercars, two of which she was too scared to drive, sat in her garage. And she'd give it all up to see Eduardo smile at her with love in his eyes just one more time.

She had to clear her throat before she could get her voice to work. "What's done is done. We can't go back. I told you I still regret it. My question to you is, can we move forward? Have you decided what to do about my … request?" Patience was not a subject taught in diva school.

He strode over to the bar in the corner and fiddled with the top of the whisky bottle before turning away empty-handed. That was Eduardo—always in control.

His face was grim when he finally looked her in the eye. "I can't make love to you, Anna. Find some other guy." A muscle throbbed in his jaw, and one fist was clenched at his side.

She wanted to argue ... persuade ... seduce. But even more, she wanted Eduardo to choose her because he still desired her as much as she did him.

Instead, she whispered, "Do you think we can at least be friends? For old times' sake?" He raised one sardonic eyebrow. "How about friendly, for Timo's sake?" she said as she heard the little boy's excited voice drift through the open terrace door.

"That, I can do."

Timo erupted onto the terrace, a cat clutched in his arms. "This place is amazing! It's even bigger than my daycare!" he shouted.

Raul followed behind, a look of consternation on his face. "I've told him this is a holiday and we're just visiting for a few days."

Anna kneeled so her face was near level with the little boy's. "Let's make this the best holiday ever," she said. "Shall we go check out the garden?"

"Can Nahla come?"

Anna glanced at the feline. It looked like it would rather be anywhere else but was too good-natured to protest much. "I think the cat would prefer to explore on her own."

Timo scrunched his face for a second then nodded, holding out the animal to Eduardo.

"Actually, the cat belongs here. I was just pet-sitting

while my friends are in France. Nahla is completely at home." He set the cat down and it quickly scampered out of sight, either to investigate its favorite haunts or avoid more over-exuberant affection.

"Do you want to come with us, Señor Forenza?" Timo asked.

Anna held her breath. She needed a little time away from the pull of Eduardo's presence to process his rejection. His refusal to relieve her of her virginity rankled. She'd nursed a secret fantasy that if he made love to her, it would obliterate the walls around his heart and they could be together once more.

Her imagination could work when it wanted to—just not when she was making hotel reservations under the influence.

Eduardo ruffled Timo's hair and muttered some excuse about needing to make a call. So she and Timo left the two men on the terrace and found a small playground set behind the rose garden. Timo ran from the slide to the monkey bars, not seeming to know where to start. After three times on the slide, including a face-first version Anna watched through her fingers, the little boy clambered onto the raised platform. He stretched, even going on tiptoe, but couldn't reach the first rung on the monkey bars. He looked pleadingly at Anna, and she quickly moved to assist him. He managed two passes with her holding his legs while he attempted to grab each successive bar.

"How's it s'posed to be done?" Timo asked.

She glanced from the quizzical face of the little boy to the bar above her head. Trips to the park had been a rarity in her childhood. This would be her first time on the play equipment. A tiny laugh escaped her. At least she'd get to try something new, even if it wasn't what she'd hoped for.

Her ponytail swung side to side as she made the return trip across the apparatus with Timo's cheers encouraging her. Glancing up, she caught Eduardo watching from an open window. Well, let him look. Let him see what could be if he'd let go of his anger and pain.

But even she wasn't enough of a dreamer to pretend that they'd have a future. Eventually, she'd leave again. She'd made a promise to Simon to oversee his foundation. She had a record contract to fulfill and fans to keep happy. She'd put too much of herself into her career to just abandon it now.

But, Dios, was one night in his arms too much to ask? What was the point in being a superstar if you couldn't get the one thing you wanted?

***

Eduardo flung back the sheet and stalked to the window. Could the woman not even allow him an hour's sleep? The practical lawyer in him reasoned that it had been more than an hour since he'd said a stilted good-night to her. A glance at the bedside clock showed it was now 3:00 a.m. Plenty of time for him to have fallen into a deep sleep and not be awakened by the faint strumming of a guitar coming from the terrace below.

Dinner had been a disaster. Raul had claimed that

Timo was tired, so the two of them ate earlier in the kitchen, leaving Eduardo alone with Anna in the massive, formal dining room. She'd worn a fitted dress that showcased her luscious curves and long, toned legs beneath its too-short hem. The soft pink color had matched the blush that infused her cheeks when she'd checked him out in his borrowed button-down shirt and slightly too-tight black pants. Tomorrow he'd have to send someone into Mendoza to get them their own wardrobes. With strict instructions that anything for Anna needed to be ugly, with full coverage.

He was so close to falling for her again. The way she interacted with Timo, the genuine warmth and affection she showed to all she encountered—this was the Anna he remembered. She'd always been kind. In his dark world of constant criticism and abuse, she'd been the one thing that made getting up in the morning worthwhile.

Was there any way they could go back to being friends, as she'd asked? His brain didn't even hesitate before throwing out the answer. It would never work. They'd never been *just friends*. From the moment he'd seen her in the community center thirteen years ago— strumming a guitar with two strings missing and a huge hole patched with duct tape—he'd been fascinated. Captivated. Enthralled.

She'd been playing a silly song to a gaggle of young children to help them remember some math formula. The lyrics had been inconsequential. Her voice, her radiance, her amazing smile—they'd transcended the mundane, decrepit building and taken him to paradise.

In that instant, his court-ordered community service had become the best thing to ever happen to him. While he assisted the aged athletics coordinator and taught younger kids the rules of various sports, Anna, out of the goodness of her heart, helped others with their homework. By the third day of his sentence, Eduardo was hopelessly in love, a punishment that lasted much longer than the four weeks he served for petty vandalism.

Within a week of meeting Anna, he took the money he'd been saving for a new pair of rugby boots and bought her a second-hand guitar for her birthday. It wasn't anything special—his father had stolen some of the cash Eduardo had saved—but at least it had all the strings and the body was intact.

Dios, the music she'd made with that thing. Every new song she sang to him first, seeking his approval. A niggle in his soul told him then that her talent would take her away. But in his youth, his stupidity, he believed he could hold her against the lure of fame and fortune.

Ironically, it was his athleticism that first tore them apart. The letter inviting him to try out for the Mendoza rugby club seemed a godsend at the time. If he made the starting fifteen, the salary would set them up for the future. And that was just the beginning. He was soon called up to play for the national team. And he was declared a hero when he scored a try in Los Pumas's one and only win over the All Blacks. European clubs called, and he was inundated with agents offering to represent him. The world was at his feet. He and Anna spent endless hours on Skype talking about the possibilities.

Those dreams were shattered by a vicious tackle and a phone call ending their relationship that still replayed in his nightmares. After he realized Anna wasn't coming back, he concentrated hard on getting a degree. Of course, without the rugby money paying his way, he had to work his ass off to keep ahead of the tuition payments.

While staying in Mendoza, he met Tiago, and their friendship led him to his current situation as partner and development director for Alva-Suarez Properties. With Tiago wanting to work less to concentrate on his family, Eduardo would soon be running the company. His plan to take it global was ambitious but doable.

However, none of it was going to happen if he was stuck out here in the countryside. The sooner they figured out who was behind the attacks, the sooner he could get back to BA, say goodbye to Anna, and launch his expansion strategy.

Right this moment, all he wanted was a few hours of sleep. When was the last time his head had been on a pillow for more than three hours? It was before Anna's reappearance in his life, that was for damn sure.

Her angelic whisper accompanied the guitar now. There'd be no chance of rest until she stopped luring him with her siren song. He tugged on Raul's oversized shirt, leaving the buttons undone, and a pair of sweatpants he'd borrowed from Tiago's closet. He headed downstairs.

Anna sat on the sofa, cross-legged, her guitar resting on her lap. A notebook and her cell phone were beside her. She was scribbling something on the paper while her left hand, reflexively it seemed, fingered silent chords on the instrument.

He remained in the shadows, absorbed in the way the moonlight caressed the waves of her blonde hair, which she'd left loose for once, and turned her skin into a pearly confection. Within a minute, however, she stilled, and her gaze probed the dark recess where he stood.

"Eduardo?" she whispered.

Moving forward into the light, he didn't miss how her breathing quickened and her nipples hardened under the thin fabric of her nightshirt. She licked her lips, and his cock stirred. His body's argument to take her, just once to relieve the ache, grew louder.

"I didn't want to interrupt you," he said.

She placed the guitar beside her on the sofa. "Sorry, did I wake you? I thought it would be quieter down here in the courtyard than in the bedroom across the hall from yours. I forgot your room probably looks out onto the terrace, doesn't it? I tried to find the study, but this house is a maze."

"Tiago's home office is on the third floor. You didn't wake me, though. I wasn't really asleep."

She nodded. "Does today's explosion keep replaying in your mind as well?"

No, but your lithe body swinging from the monkey bars does. "Yes. Is that what your song is about?"

"No." She glanced at the paper then back at him. "May I play it for you? It's currently titled 'Memory Palace.'"

His inner voice shrieked at him to escape before he lost what little remained of his self-control. Stupid voice.

From the second he'd left his bedroom to seek her out, his sane, rational side had abandoned him as a lost cause. Afraid of what might come out of his mouth, he simply sat across from her and nodded.

That guitar. It couldn't be … could it?

She picked up the slightly battered but obviously well-loved instrument. After strumming a few opening chords, her eyes captured and held his prisoner. Her voice joined with the melody, not quite a whisper but the perfect pitch to steal into his heart and scatter the few pieces he'd managed to cement back together.

> They say if you want to remember
> Important things in life
> You should build a palace in your mind
> And fill it with your life
>
> So I built myself a palace
> A place within my mind
> A whole wing is dedicated to you
> Crammed with all you meant to me
>
> As I walk the halls of my palace
> I have come to realize
> Whole floors of rooms are empty
> After you, I forgot to live my life
>
> There is no children's laughter
> No baby's first cries or smiles
> I can't bear to visit your wing

I had to lock it from my mind

The place where love should linger
Is empty of your voice
No laughs or hugs or baby kisses
Can comfort me when I cry

As I walk the halls of my palace
I have come to realize
Whole floors of rooms are empty
After you, I forgot to live my life

My palace is cold and lonely
Footsteps echo in the hall
No kings or queens cavort or dance
It's really no fun at all

As I walk the halls of my palace
I have come to realize
Whole floors of rooms are empty
After you, I forgot to live my life

Forgot to live my life

Her voice was strong but laced with the pain clearly etched on her face.

The numbness he'd wrapped around himself since their talk this afternoon weakened, allowing the heartache of the past to penetrate once more. He'd always blamed her for leaving him. But he could see now that he'd done nothing to fight for their love. It was another failure to add to his list.

The last note drifted up into the black night to join the stars and other celestial objects.

"It's not done yet," she said after a long moment. "It still needs … something."

He cleared his throat. "How can you do this—lay bare your heart, your soul, for everyone?"

"Because it helps. Keeping it all bottled up only makes it harder. Plus, I get lots of letters and emails telling me how my songs express exactly what others are feeling. They can cope better with their problems as well."

"I'm glad our failed relationship has benefited so many. Especially your bank account."

Anger blazed in her eyes. "It's nothing like that. I sing about what's in my heart. I can't help it that you're always there."

He looked away. And the silence lengthened between them.

"If I'm in your heart, how could you marry someone else?"

Her voice soft, she replied, "Love had nothing to do with my marriage. I knew Simon was dying before we wed. I knew he'd never be a husband in the full sense of the word. I didn't want that. What I did want was a break from all the speculation about my sexuality and lack of relationships. He wanted a companion in his last days, someone he could trust. For all he'd done for me since I went to America… For all the support he'd given me, I wanted to be the one who held his hand when the pain got too much. The one who sat by his bedside and sang softly to him when he couldn't sleep. And you know what, Eduardo? I have no regrets about marrying him. I'd do it again in a heartbeat."

"Your marriage nearly destroyed me." All the emotion she'd poured into her song he now released. "Dios. You'd already been gone for six years. I thought I was over you. But when the photos of you in your wedding dress appeared on the television screen while I was watching the news … I drank for two days solid. I became my father. If Tiago hadn't sobered me up, I'd be sitting in an alley somewhere now."

"No." Her harsh word brought his gaze back to hers. "You wouldn't. You're the strongest person I know. Just because you had a minor setback doesn't mean you're weak. It means you're human."

How could she still do that? She made him feel better with just a few words, spoken with the confidence of someone who knew everything about him and still liked what they saw.

She set the guitar down, and this time he was sure it was the same one he'd bought her all those years ago. She had money now. Why did she keep that old piece of garbage? His heart offered up an answer, but his mind rejected it. Must be a musician's superstition at work. Because she'd had a hit with the first song she'd written on the instrument, she kept using it.

She stood. The moonlight behind her appeared like a halo around her head, but his reaction was anything but heavenly. There was no disguising the waves of desire that swirled between them.

"Can I ask one thing of you?" she whispered.

The hairs on his nape stood on end. "You can ask." At least his inner lawyer hadn't entirely abandoned him.

"Will you kiss me? Just once. I need to know if it is as good as I remember, or if I've just imagined the bliss."

A logical request. And one he'd contemplated more than once in the dark of the night in his lonely bed. Neither the lawyer nor the romantic within him offered any input. They were curious as well.

He stood so he was in the position of power, able to walk away if necessary. "For the record, I don't think this is a good idea."

"Noted." Her hands were already on his bare chest, slowly inching their way up. He shivered as her fingers skimmed over his collarbone. Her gaze shot to his. "I want to kiss your injury."

"Another bad idea," he murmured but did nothing to stop her as she slid the shirt from his shoulders. He flung it off, tossing it towards the sofa where she'd sung of everything they'd lost. The night air cooled his overheated skin.

"Noted again." This time when her fingers flitted up his chest, her touch was electric, energizing every nerve ending, sending jolts of electricity south to his groin. "Your body is amazing." Her whisper against his skin flash-fried any resistance his common sense attempted to mount in defense.

He held himself rigid under the sensuous torture of her lips and tongue as they worked their way from one end of his clavicle to the other.

"Anna…" *Dios*. Was that his voice?

Her answer was to pull his head down and touch his lips with hers. For an eternity, she kept still and just rested their mouths together. Then her tongue traced the seam of his lips, and it was more than he could resist.

His hands reached for her hips and he pulled her against him. Ten years melted away. Except now the eagerness of youth was enhanced with experience. A sigh escaped. A moan of pleasure. Heartbeats accelerated, and touches became more insistent, more frantic.

Finally, they broke apart, their chests heaving. The dazed look in Anna's eyes was surely reflected in his.

Damn. This was not good.

Chapter Seven

It would have been so much easier if the embrace had been mediocre. If she'd built up the—well, there was no other word for it—awesomeness in her mind. If Eduardo didn't make every cell in her body light up like Times Square on New Year's Eve. But he did.

Worse. *Only* he did.

He'd been the first boy to kiss her. But since then she'd had dozens of men try. Some physically more attractive, models and Hollywood heartthrobs; many musicians with whom she shared a kindred spirit; many actors with whom she'd shared romantic scenes in her videos. Not a single one compared to the way Eduardo made her feel.

The way he made her feel too much.

"Well, that answers that question," she said. "Not the answer either of us had hoped for, I'm guessing."

"Like I said, bad idea."

She huffed out a laugh. At least Eduardo looked like the rug had been yanked out from beneath him as well. "Yeah. But it had to be done."

"Did it?" He ran his hands through his hair, and she rubbed her fingers together, remembering the silkiness. "Are we any better off? Nothing can come of this … this chemistry between us."

And that was probably one of the world's great tragedies. They could be burning up the sheets, making each other feel amazing. Instead they stood on a terrace in the dark, throbbing with need, heading to their own separate beds.

"I know." She ran the heel of her palm over her sternum. "I'd better get to sleep or I'll shock everyone with the way I look tomorrow. Last thing I need is photos of me looking a mess being leaked to the press."

"Why would that be so bad? Is looking beautiful the only thing that matters to you?"

"No, of course not. It's the speculation about *why* I'm a mess that does my head in. Is it drugs? Alcohol? Six men and a hairy he-goat in my bed the previous night?"

"Really? Ménage and bestiality at the same time?"

"The tabloid press have vivid imaginations."

"Well, you don't have to worry about photos being leaked as long as you're here. Tiago's staff are very discreet, and they've been warned that if anyone even hints you're in residence, they will be instantly dismissed and prosecuted."

"Harsh."

"I'm trying to protect you."

She wiped both hands over her face. Even then she could still feel where Eduardo's fingers had touched her cheeks. "I know. I'm just tired and on edge. Thank you."

He nodded, but his movements were stilted, like he was holding onto his control by a fingernail. "I'll have someone go into town tomorrow to buy some clothes for us. If you can make a list of anything else you need or want, it would be helpful."

"How long do you think we'll be here?"

"Expect to stay at least a week. Maybe two."

"Two weeks? I can't disappear that long. The press will have a field day."

"Dios! Someone is trying to kill one of us, and all you can think about is what the media will report."

"I've given ten years of my life and sacrificed everything for my career. So, yeah, I'm a little concerned about things that will affect it." It was all she had now. Possibly all she'd ever have, given that Eduardo was the only one who could turn off her let-me-just-overthink-this button with a simple kiss.

"I'm no happier than you. I've got properties to investigate and contracts to negotiate. But if we don't stay here, the media may be reporting one of our deaths."

That put it into perspective. "Fine. I'll have my admin team release more photos of me in various European cities so everyone thinks I'm holidaying there."

"Good idea. Just don't tell them where you really are. Be brief and use the house phone, not your cell, when you call. Tiago has a secure line in his home office. And make sure the location service is turned off on all your devices. That won't slow down a professional hit man, but why make it easier for them?"

"I will. Good night then, Eduardo."

He seemed about to say something but instead clenched his hands into fists at his side. "Don't forget your guitar," he finally managed.

"I wouldn't ever forget it." She snagged the

instrument and fled upstairs to her room. Her grip on the fingerboard tight enough to embed string marks on her palm. What did she expect? That he'd declare his love and his desire to follow her around the world as she toured and lived out her dreams, just because they'd kissed again?

She wrote out her shopping list and slipped it under Eduardo's bedroom door. No light escaped the portal. Had he come up and gone straight to sleep? Or was he still down on the terrace, rooted to the spot where, for a few brief minutes, they'd time-traveled back ten years?

She slid between her own sheets. Regret, her constant companion, gave her the cold shoulder.

It was bright when she woke. The mountains in the distance stood like sentinels. Today she was going to pull it all together and formulate a plan. She couldn't stay here with Eduardo for two weeks and maintain any semblance of indifference. She could just as easily hide out in America. Perhaps one of the elite commandos Eduardo had hired to guard the place could escort her back to LA. The only good thing she could say about the current situation was that it had awakened her muse. She needed to get these emotions on paper before they festered inside her.

Yes, that's what she needed to do: get back to work. She'd find Eduardo and tell him of her decision. Right after breakfast. Or, glancing at the clock, lunch, since it was nearly noon. At least the bags under her eyes had been unpacked. Seven hours of sleep was a new record for her.

A shower restored more of her mental alertness.

And despite Eduardo's assurance that the staff wouldn't take photos of her, she carefully applied the little bit of makeup she carried in her handbag. Her hair she pulled again into a high ponytail, liking the instant energy it brought to her appearance. Undoubtedly, he would try to talk her out of leaving; she needed to look her best to give her the confidence to battle on an equal footing.

After a quick sandwich in the kitchen, eaten while the cook regaled her with stories of a niece who had posters of Angel plastered all over her room, Anna went in search of Eduardo. He'd said the home office was on the third floor, so that seemed the most likely place to find him.

His voice was muffled through the wood-paneled door. She knocked in case he was in a meeting or on a private phone call, but his "enter" came almost immediately.

She pushed open the door and came to an abrupt halt. Her jaw joined her internal organs on the floor. Eduardo was naked from the waist up, his pants hanging low on his ass. Another man was dabbing something on the millions of lacerations on Eduardo's back. As he turned his head, exhaustion and pain were clearly etched on his too-handsome face, and there was a worrying pallor to his skin. Still, a small smile creased his lips as his gaze swept her up and down. She'd pulled on pair of her absent hostess's white capris and a navy blue crop top, leaving her stomach visible.

"I thought you were the housekeeper," Eduardo said by way of greeting. "I asked her to get a new shirt for me." He tilted his head towards the man still dabbing antiseptic on his wounds. "This is Dr. Salvio. Doctor, this is Anna Marquez."

The physician spared her a quick glance but made no sign he recognized her as anyone special. Which, today, she wasn't. Guilt ate a hole in her stomach while that organ bungee-jumped within her. She'd been so caught up in her own situation that she'd neglected to realize Eduardo was seriously hurt.

"Why didn't you tell me you were badly injured?" Damn the man. Was he so intent on keeping her shut out of his life he couldn't even share this with her? She blinked back the ridiculous moisture gathering in her eyes.

"Raul dressed the cuts yesterday after we arrived. I called the doctor today only out of an abundance of caution. I'll be no good at protecting you if I'm delirious with an infection-induced fever."

"Forget protecting me. You need to look after yourself."

Another knock sounded on the still-open door; the housekeeper held up a brown button-up shirt on a hanger.

"*Gracias*, Rosa. Please put it on the sofa," Eduardo said.

As the woman moved to do as he asked, Anna took in the rest of the room. Dark wood paneling and a burgundy leather sofa declared this a masculine domain. But the cream curtains, throw pillows, and a few silver-framed family photos spoke of a feminine influence. Right now, along with Eduardo's shirt, bags from various chain stores littered the sofa's cushions.

"There's your new wardrobe. Sorry, no designer stuff. Purchases in high-end stores would have aroused suspicion. Slumming it in regular clothes won't hurt you for a week or two."

If he weren't injured before, he would be now. She strode towards him. "How dare you—"

"Easy, *querida*..." His cheeky grin turned into a wince as the doctor treated a particularly deep cut. "I only said that because I much prefer the fire in your eyes."

Bastard. She turned back to the sofa to rummage through the bags. T-shirts, jeans, a couple of long skirts, and a few silky tops. She pulled out a maxi dress with a bold geometric pattern in red and yellow. Angel's personal shopper would never have chosen any of these items. Which made them even better. Having spent years being told what to wear to keep her image intact, breaking free and wearing things just because they were pretty was liberating.

"Everything is perfect. Who do I owe and how much?"

"We'll settle accounts at the end of your stay."

That sounded ominous. The last line to the song 'Hotel California' flitted through her mind. She could check out anytime, but would she be allowed to leave?

"There," the doctor said as he taped the last bandage in place. "Keep the area dry, take the antibiotics I gave you, and try to sleep. You won't heal if you keep pushing yourself. I'll check on you in two days."

Eduardo refastened his pants then moved over to the sofa, reaching past her to snag the shirt the housekeeper had left there. He shrugged it on, his face paling even more as it pulled across his back, making the dark shadows under his eyes more prominent. He didn't bother to button it.

"When's the last time you slept?" she demanded after the doctor left.

A self-depreciating laugh escaped Eduardo's lips. "When did you arrive back in my life?"

"You haven't slept since Monday?"

"I've had a lot on my mind."

She pulled in a deep breath. History was about to repeat itself—he was injured and she was leaving. But it had to be done. "Let me eliminate one worry. I want to go back to America." He opened his mouth, and she put up a hand. "Hear me out first. You say you've got an elite team of commandos surrounding this place. Well, assign one or two to escort me back to LA. I'll hire a private plane and have a security team meet us in the States. They can look after me from there. I'll cover all the expenses. That way, if it's discovered that I'm the target, you won't have to put your life on hold any longer. And in the meantime, I can get back to work."

"No."

"Excuse me? When were you appointed my overlord?"

"The first time I met your grandmother." He started to cross his arms over his chest but, with a grimace, settled for shoving his hands into the front pockets of his jeans.

"Explain."

"Do you remember the day you brought me home

to meet your family?"

"Of course." She'd been so excited, clutching his hand with both of hers and smiling up at him as though he were her whole world.

"Do you remember your grandmother sending you out to buy some cola?"

"Yeah." To have pop had been a rarity. But her first boyfriend was considered worthy of a celebration. Except in her mother's eyes. The next day she'd been marched down to the clinic and put on a contraceptive pill. *Madre* was not going to have Anna repeating her mistake.

"While you were out, your grandmother sat me down and said that as you had no father in your life, my role as your first boyfriend was crucial. She said the way I treated you would be the benchmark for all future relationships you had with men. If I treated you well, cared for you, protected you, and didn't allow my own desires to come before what was best for you, every man you met afterward would have to live up to the same standards. It was a hell of a load to bear, but for you, I was willing to take on that responsibility—even though I naïvely assured your grandmother that I was going to be the only man in your life. She made me swear on your life that I would protect you, even from myself."

"Is that why you wouldn't make love to me when we were teens?"

"Yes."

She pulled in a deep breath despite a tight chest. "Abuela's dead now. You're released from your vow."

A wry smile twisted his lips. "And yet here I am,

still wanting to protect you. Except now it seems to be from yourself. There was no release clause in my vow to your grandmother. I promised forever."

"I'm no longer fifteen, Eduardo. I thank you for your service, but your time as protector and boyfriend role model is over. I'm going back to America."

He glanced out the window for a moment. "What if I told you that I've rethought my position on helping you with your … problem?"

"You're willing to have sex with me?"

"Yes. If the offer is still open."

Like that door was ever going to close.

But she wouldn't appear too eager. "What about your promise to my abuela?"

"Let's just say, I've managed to convince myself that if you're going to take lovers, I should at least show you how a woman should be respected and treated. It will be my one last role to model."

She'd got what she wanted. The key would be not wanting beyond that.

***

"When? Tonight?" The eagerness in Anna's face accelerated his heart rate.

But his hunger was tempered. He'd never been anyone's first.

"No. Not tonight. I don't want my injuries to hinder my performance and thus your pleasure. If we're going to do this, we're going to do it right. I'm not going to bend you over this desk and take you with my pants around my ankles."

A fire lit in her eyes, corresponding to a heat within him. "Shame. I was looking forward to some reckless passion."

"Passion, yes. Reckless, no." At least not the first time.

Fool, it's supposed to be just the once.

But not even his stern lawyer side could promise that when eventually he had her naked, he'd have her only the one time. If he was to be the role model for her future lovers, he'd have to do a thorough job. Even if his gut churned at the thought of her sleeping with other men.

"Well, this had better not be some ploy just to keep me here. If you don't make love to me by Sunday, then I'm gone. And I'll send my grandmother back to haunt you."

"She'd have to get in line."

Anna tilted her head but let the comment pass. "I do have one more request." She tossed the dress she'd been crushing in her hands for the past ten minutes back onto the pile of clothes. He couldn't wait to see her wear "regular people" clothes. Then she'd really be back to his Anna. Dios, he needed to stop thinking this way.

"What's your request?" The lawyer side of him was finally waking up.

"While we're waiting for you to heal, we…"

"We what?"

"We go back to the way it used to be between us. We hold hands and touch each other and kiss and take things close to the edge. That way, when we do make love, it won't be so … clinical."

His bark of laughter held no humor. "If you think my lovemaking will be clinical, let me set the record straight right now. I will have you writhing with passion, moaning my name, screaming as you climax."

A flush crept up her cheeks. "Still… Will you give me the 'boyfriend experience,' I think they call it?"

"Do you know what you're asking of me?" She wanted more than just his body. She wanted his heart and soul.

"Yes. And it's nothing more than I'm willing to give to you."

Dios, he must be tired. Or else he'd never agree to this. "All right. But starting tonight. I'm going to take a couple of painkillers and see if I can pass out for a few hours." Because heaven knew he was going to need all the restraint he could muster to keep this thing between them just physical.

"Then let me send you to bed with sweet dreams." She sauntered over, the sway of her hips enough to make a man dizzy. Her fingers brushed aside the front panels of his shirt and flitted over his nipples. Did she have any idea what she did to him?

He groaned, capturing her hands before she could do further damage. "I need to sleep, *querida*, not toss and turn in frustration."

"Can I at least kiss you?"

Yes, yes, yes. He released her hands and she cupped his face, her fingers sliding across his cheeks like a feather to slip into his hair, guiding his head down to hers. She stood on tiptoe, her body pressed against his for stability. Another soft moan escaped his lips seconds before hers settled on them.

The kiss she gave was not one of passion but of promise. Still equally devastating. "Sleep well. And heal fast. I've got plans for you," she whispered against his lips before stepping back.

Without another word, she gathered up the clothes and bags and left the room. He ran his hands through his hair to remove the tingle left by her touch. Soon, his whole body would become her playground.

This had not been his intention when he'd climbed out of bed this morning after yet another sleepless night. He'd come to the same conclusion Anna had: she was better off in America. No threats or incidents had happened there. She'd be safe.

His sanity would also be safe. He could tell himself all he wanted that he didn't sleep because of worry over the community center development. Or because his back pained him too much. The kick-in-the-balls reality was that he was too wound up about Anna. As soon as he slid between the sheets, he imagined her there with him, and all the things he wanted to do with her. It was impossible to sleep.

She'd offered the perfect solution to facilitate her return to the United States, and all he could think was that he couldn't let her go. This time she'd leave on his terms. They'd part in such a way that they could both move on with their lives in a healthy manner.

The song she'd written and sung to him the night before, about the normal family life she'd sacrificed… Well, he still wanted those things. Eventually. He wanted children. He wanted a wife to cherish and hold in the night. He wanted what he'd never had except for that brief time with Anna. He wanted love.

Tiago would pass out laughing if he discovered this admission. Eduardo had mercilessly teased that self-proclaimed bachelor-for-life when he'd fallen in love with his bride of convenience.

But if Eduardo took Anna to bed, would any other woman compare afterward? Last night's kiss had shown him that their passion still blazed strong. He prided himself on his control. Even that seemed to disappear when Anna's lips touched his. She, and she alone, swept him into a maelstrom of desire, want, need, until he wasn't sure of anything—except she was the woman he loved.

Still loved.

Kick-in-the-nuts reality at its finest.

There was no future for them. She had her singing career. He had his plans. And never the twain would meet.

He risked more heartache if he made love to her.

But neither could he walk away.

Chapter Eight

Eduardo rolled onto his side, hissing in a deep breath as the cuts on his shoulder made contact with the mattress. What time was it? He'd gone to bed at 2:00 p.m., but based on the lack of light at the edges of the curtains, it was night now. More than night, the bedside clock revealed. Almost dawn. He'd slept for sixteen hours.

Those were some pills the doctor had given him. But it wasn't the tablets that had calmed his mind. It was finally having made a decision about Anna. Taking her to bed now seemed the smart thing to do. They'd both get what they wanted. And if a weekend of sex allowed him the closure he needed to move on, that's what he'd do.

Score one for logic.

Now all he had to concentrate on was keeping his emotions in check. The thought of spending a couple of days in bed with a woman had never filled him with such elation and trepidation at the same time. He was being ridiculous. How good could it be?

If they were going to have a few days to concentrate on nothing but her sexual education, he needed to clear up a few things first. Like who was behind the attacks.

He listened to his voicemail messages, several from the office updating him on various projects, which thankfully, seemed to be running smoothly despite his absence. There was one from his contact on the police force.

They'd ruled out Raul as the target. Evidently, there was a cop undercover within the gang who said there was no vendetta against the former member. As long as Raul stayed away from criminal activity, they'd leave him alone.

Eduardo couldn't wait to tell his friend. Maybe Raul would want to relocate to Mendoza permanently once they'd settled the custody dispute. He didn't really need a driver. Tiago was always looking for good workers, and Timo seemed to love the being in the country. It could be good for both father and son to have a fresh start.

On to the other avenues of inquiry. Eduardo did a quick time difference calculation, then placed a call to his friend and business partner on holiday in France.

"You okay?" Tiago asked as he answered the phone.

"Yeah, a few cuts and bruises but nothing serious. Thanks again for letting us hide out at your place and for the use of your plane."

"It might be clichéd, but it's still true: *mi casa es su casa*. How are the other guests?"

"Fine. Little Timo loves it here. We may have a hard time getting him to leave." He was not going to discuss Anna. His friend was too astute. He'd recognize the change in Eduardo's voice when he even said her name.

"You can all stay as long as required."

"Thanks." He needed to switch subjects before his throat closed. "About the community center—"

"You think I'm worried about the company when someone blew up my best friend's car?"

That elicited a genuine chuckle. "My, how the mighty have fallen. I recall a time not too long ago when you breathed business."

"I was a fool."

A condition Eduardo was perilously close to emulating. "Nevertheless, buildings are waiting to be built. Love may make the world go around, but it doesn't file permit applications or arrange deliveries of cement."

"No, that's what competent staff do. Let them prove themselves, Eduardo. You don't need to oversee everything. Figure out who's got a grudge against you or your friends. Then we'll sort out the rest together."

"Speaking of grudges, what have you been able to discover about Spencer and Linda Suarez?" Those two had put Tiago through hell when they'd been battling over custody of Miranda. Perhaps with their main target out of the country, they'd decided to focus their revenge on Eduardo, who'd helped thwart their plans.

"Spencer is still in prison in Rawson. He's had a few visitors lately. We're making inquiries. Linda is in BA, on parole. But according to the officer assigned to her, she's been a model citizen."

"The woman is a snake. I wouldn't trust her with a rotten apple."

"Agreed. I've got someone tailing her, but so far she hasn't done anything suspicious."

Eduardo groaned. This tangle had so many threads it was going to take more than one lead to figure out who was involved.

"Jacques has been dealing with the American suspects. Do you want to talk to him?"

"Please, if he's available."

"He's right here. We were discussing a collaboration with our vineyards."

"*Bonjour*, Eduardo," Jacques de Launay, Tiago's pseudo half brother greeted him. The man was a billionaire who'd left it all behind to go into hiding with the woman he loved because of a threat on her life. If anyone understood Eduardo's position, it was Jacques.

"I appreciate your help," Eduardo began.

"No problem. To be honest, since Maya's troubles are over, things have been a bit dull."

"At the moment, I'd gladly take dull. Have you uncovered anything?"

"Your woman has an interesting family."

Eduardo let the comment about Anna being his woman pass. "I know her late husband's children are suing her for a larger share of the estate. But Anna doesn't believe they're capable of violence."

"That was my investigator's initial assessment as well. In her words, 'they couldn't find their way out of a closet.' The likelihood of them organizing an escalating terror campaign is highly improbable. But that doesn't mean there isn't someone in the background who has the wherewithal to do it. The instigator might benefit if any of those three came into a lot of money."

"That's a possibility." And it widened the search even more. *Mierda.*

"Another person of interest is Anna's mother."

Eduardo sat. "Valentina? Why would she want to

endanger her own daughter?" They didn't have the closest relationship—at least they hadn't when Anna had been his girlfriend. And given Anna's response when he'd asked about her mother, it hadn't improved in the meantime.

"Valentina Marquez, now Fuller, is deeply in debt, and her marriage is on the rocks. Anna pays her a monthly stipend, but it's obviously not enough for the lifestyle she's living. Maybe she's hoping that if her daughter is upset, she'll turn to her mother for comfort and get back into her good books. Or worse. Ask Anna if her mother is a beneficiary in her will. Valentina could have approximately a hundred and fifty million reasons to want her daughter dead."

Eduardo rubbed his sternum. This would crush Anna. Her mother was all she had left. "I'll ask her about their relationship and the terms of her will."

"*Très bien*. We'll keep investigating. I'll pass you back to Tiago. Good luck and stay safe, Eduardo."

"Thanks again, Jacques."

Tiago came back on the line. "Hey, I just wanted to let you know we're heading back early. We'll arrive in Mendoza on Sunday."

"You're not cutting short your holiday because of me, are you?" Was this sinking feeling consternation that his friend had curtailed his vacation? Or disappointment that he now wouldn't be spending an entire two days in bed with Anna?

"No. As I mentioned, Jacques and I are going to co-produce a vintage next year. He wants to taste the grapes personally, and they need to travel soon as Maya is getting big with the twins she's expecting. He doesn't want to leave her or have her travel any closer to her due date."

Another man so besotted with his wife he couldn't bear to be apart from her for even a few days. A vision of Anna pregnant with his child flitted through Eduardo's mind. Nope, he wouldn't be able to travel solo either.

"Okay. See you Sunday."

The pressure on his chest increased. If he let himself fantasize about a future with Anna and what they could mean to each other, he'd stare heartache in the face again.

He needed to exercise, clear his body of the pain meds, and get his focus back.

He downed the glass of water beside the bed and brushed his teeth to rid his mouth of the woolly sensation. After slipping on a pair of shorts, he exited his room.

And ran straight into Anna.

***

Eduardo's strong hands grabbed her arms or she would have fallen.

"Sorry. I didn't expect you to be outside my bedroom door at six in the morning," he said.

Busted. Heat crept up her neck, infusing her cheeks. "I heard your voice and I was worried. You slept so long. Raul checked on you twice, just to make sure you were still breathing." She searched his face, looking for signs of fever or delirium. She hadn't been able to hear what he said, but she was concerned. Had he been talking in his sleep or hallucinating that someone was with him?

"I was on my phone. Those pills really knocked me out. But I'm feeling better now. I was just going for a run."

"Is that wise? The doctor told you to keep your back dry. I don't think getting all sweaty will help you heal."

"Damn, I had forgotten that. I'll just walk around the gardens. Some fresh air will clear my head of the pain pills."

Wow, was he desperate to get away from her or what?

"Outside? In the dark? And have the commandos shoot you, thinking you're an intruder?"

He rubbed his hand over his chin, now sporting two days' growth of beard. Dios, he was so sexy. "Not likely, but I take your point."

"There's a fully equipped fitness room on the ground floor. You could walk on the treadmill. Just give me a second to change."

His eyes flitted down her body, pausing where her breasts pressed against the thin cotton camisole she wore. Under his gaze, her nipples pebbled. And that had nothing on the moisture gathering between her thighs.

"I don't need a nanny, Anna. I'll see you at breakfast." He turned to leave.

"Eduardo." She grabbed his arm, and his muscles tensed beneath her fingers. "I…"

How did you explain to someone so self-sufficient—someone who'd had no one to rely on since childhood—that you were lonely? While he slept, she'd spent the day rattling around this big house. She'd wanted to play with Timo, but he'd been helping his father wash Tiago's seemingly endless inventory of vehicles. The pride and joy on the little boy's face as he scrubbed at the rims of a Bentley with an old toothbrush had been too precious to interrupt.

Still, the emptiness in her life echoed around her soul. She had no right to burden Eduardo with her drama. That didn't mean she couldn't try to cajole him into a small display of affection, something to get her through the next few hours.

"You promised me the boyfriend experience," she blurted out.

His eyes narrowed and his chest expanded as he pulled in a deep breath. "Even when we were together, we didn't live in each other's pockets. I just want to exercise. I promise not to do anything too strenuous."

"All right. But how about a see-you-later kiss?"

The words had barely left her mouth before he'd wrapped a strong arm around her waist and pulled her against him. His other hand gently tilted her face up. Passion darkened his eyes to nearly black, but they were softened by some other emotion she dared not name. The second his lips touched hers, however, her eyes drifted closed. She'd been chilled standing in the hallway wearing only a camisole and shorts. Now heat engulfed her, and even those few scraps of fabric seemed too much.

Her back hit the wall and Eduardo's hand at her waist slid under her thigh and pulled it up to anchor around his hips. His touch was fire, and she burned inside and out. *Madre de Dios*, this was just a kiss. When he did make love to her, she'd be a puddle in seconds. Her head filled with his scent of bergamot and sandalwood, drowning her in want. He tasted of minty toothpaste and the essence of Eduardo. She couldn't get enough.

His mouth devoured hers. This was no gentle kiss. No embrace between teenagers exploring their sexuality for the first time. This was a man who knew how to make a woman writhe with passion, as he'd promised. His tongue swept against hers, dueling, leaving her in no doubt of his expertise. The hand at the back of her knee slid along her inner thigh. If his fingers slipped five centimeters to the left, he'd find her soaking wet and ready for him.

A gasp escaped her lips as his other hand slid under her top and caressed her bare breast. He rolled her tight nipple between his thumb and index finger, giving it a gentle pull. She nearly came out of her skin. Every single one of her nerve endings was alive, waiting, begging for his next touch. His teeth nipped her bottom lip before sucking it into his mouth, soothing the minor sting with a caress of his tongue.

Her head fell backward and hit the wall when he abandoned her mouth and traced his way across her jaw and down the corded side of her neck with little nips and licks.

His index finger followed the seam of her shorts between her legs, and she could feel him smile against the skin of her collarbone. His hand cupped her full breast, which pulsed with need. Her fingers in his hair tried to tug his mouth down to her chest. She wanted his tongue on her nipples more than she needed to breathe.

Instead he returned his lips to hers and once more plundered what she willingly offered. Her senses were overloaded, firing messages too fast for her brain to comprehend. Each sweep of his fingers over her flesh sent a cascade of electric shocks through her system. The world, her problems, her fears, all disappeared under his skill.

This. *This* was what she'd missed by choosing her career over love.

He released her lips.

"Edio." His nickname escaped her mouth, accompanied by a breathy moan. He licked the shell of her ear, melting her bones. It was several seconds before she realized that both her feet were back on the ground. Her top had been tugged down, but his hands were on her hips only, to steady her.

"Go back to bed, Anna. I'll see you at breakfast," he whispered into her ear, his hot breath sliding down her neck to nestle between her breasts. Too soon he broke even that contact, moving to the middle of the hallway and leaving a lifetime of distance between them. If it weren't for the rapid rise and fall of his chest and the discernible bulge in the front of his shorts, she'd never believe he'd been involved in the most passionate encounter of her life.

"Eduardo." How could he just walk away after … that?

"Later we need to talk about your mother," he said

striding down the hall towards the stairs.

No other eight words could have doused her ardor as quickly.

She sank to the floor. Her back against the wall was the only thing keeping her upright. Her brain was still befuddled and couldn't send the necessary messages to her legs to carry her to her bedroom. Not that she'd be able to sleep anyway. She may never sleep again until he finished what he started.

This was not what she'd expected. Sure, the passion was more than anything she'd ever known, but she'd been quasi-prepared for that. It was the need for him. Not just for his body. For all of him. Every single piece of his body, heart, mind, and soul. She craved it all.

Eventually, she picked herself up off the floor and made her way back to her room. Her bed was too big, too lonely to even contemplate a return there. Instead she sat on the round armchair and pulled her guitar into her lap. The familiar pose soothed her soul as her fingers picked out chords at random, stringing sounds together that reflected the chaos of her heart.

Had she made a huge mistake in trying to reignite the flame between her and Eduardo?

She needed to tread carefully. Love for him still lingered in her heart. But she'd lost a lot of people she loved recently; she was emotionally bereft. And at a low point in her career. Add in an intense attraction that had never died, and she could so easily fall back to into the submissive girlfriend role. That wouldn't do. Not only would it be cheating herself, it would be unfair to Eduardo too. He deserved a strong woman who could stand on her own and support him in times of difficulty. She still wanted him to make love to her—*Dios*, she wanted him, especially after that kiss—but anything more than that would have to wait until she was at a better place in her life.

She loved being Angel, sharing her talent with the world, helping people cope with their own emotional turmoil, but she was realizing she also loved being Anna. How long had it been since she'd played with a child as she'd done with Timo the other day? How long since she'd worn clothes in bright, fun colors that didn't come with a designer name attached? How long since she'd laughed until she snorted? Angel never snort-laughed.

That was going to change. Starting now. She'd find a balance between her life and her career. Then go after everything she wanted.

That they *did* teach in diva school.

***

Not being able to pound his body into submission was damned annoying. Eduardo did his lower body workout, but the lunges weren't cutting it to dampen his ardor. What the hell had he been thinking, kissing Anna that way? He hadn't been thinking at all. The hallway incident had been entirely hormonal, a lust-hazed action-adventure of epic proportions. Incredible. And anything but wise.

No jury of his peers would convict him of taking things too far too fast when faced with a partially clad woman who held his heart in her clenched fist and demanded that he kiss her. Hell, she'd been with him every step of the way.

The problem was his lack of self-control. It had all been too amazing, too scorching, too … emotional. Her response, her touch, her taste had overwhelmed him until he'd been reduced to a man whose sole purpose was to give pleasure. And receive it. Dios, she'd been so hot.

Maybe he shouldn't have run his fingers along her inner thigh or stroked between her legs. Even through the layers of fabric, her heat had enticed him to strip the shorts from her body and plunge into her wetness. He'd been stopped only by the flashing reminder that she was a virgin and her first time should be more than a pounding against the wall in his friend's hallway.

Lust flamed again within him. This was going to be a hell of a few days if he could neither act on the desire nor alleviate it with exercise. He should stay away from her. Not that that was an option. She wanted the boyfriend experience. Maybe this morning's demonstration showed he wasn't boyfriend material.

He tried to recall his vow to her grandmother. It had kept him in check in the past. Unfortunately, he was no longer dealing with a teenage girl on the cusp of womanhood. Anna was one-hundred-percent temptress.

The only benefit from the early morning escapade was that his heart rate had been accelerated enough that he didn't need to do a warm-up before exercising. And by the time he'd hit the gym, the drugs were gone from his system.

Raul joined him a few minutes later. If he noticed his boss's rather desperate demeanor, he said nothing.

Eduardo caught Raul's gaze. "It wasn't your past catching up with you in BA. The gang says as long as you stay out of their business, they'll leave you alone."

"I'm glad it wasn't because of me. I was trying to figure out how I'd pay you back for your car."

"Insurance will do that. There was something else I wanted to ask. How would you feel about relocating here to Mendoza?"

A smile lit the other man's face. "You're moving here? Timo loves seeing the mountains and all the green fields. Of course, he's going to be disappointed that we won't be living in a grand place like this, but I think the change will do him good. I swear he's already grown an inch in the few days we've been here. But that could be all the treats the cook is feeding him."

"No, I'm not moving. But I know Tiago is looking for a warehouse manager. I could recommend you. He has great plans for the winery. It could be a stepping-stone to an interesting career for you."

The smile faded from Raul's eyes. "I have no experience."

"I wouldn't say that. You ran a very efficient product distribution network for the cartel. This job would be similar, just more legal."

"But you…"

Eduardo put his hand on the big man's shoulder. "*Amigo*, we both know I don't really need a driver. And that you are capable of so much more. I would hate for you to look back on your life in ten years and feel you've wasted it behind the wheel." Eduardo read reluctant acknowledgment in the other man's eyes. But he couldn't limit his friend's potential because Raul felt indebted. "Besides, I don't currently have a car for you to drive. Mine got blown up, if you recall."

"I don't know…"

"Just think about it. We still have to wrap up the custody case. But with what I've been able to uncover about your ex-wife, I'm pretty sure you'll be granted full custody. And if we can tell the judge you have a good job and a healthy environment for Timo here in Mendoza, that will also go in your favor. Tiago will be home on Sunday. Meet with him and see if you like the sound of the job, and if you could work with him."

There was a glassiness in Raul's eyes. Eduardo moved over to the rack to pull off a couple of dumbbells, giving his friend a chance to get his emotions under control. Eduardo attempted a bicep curl but stopped when the skin across his back protested. He did not want to risk a delay in recovery if it meant he'd have to wait longer to make love to Anna.

"Why?" Raul asked. His voice held a hint of a quaver, and he cleared it. "Why are you doing all this for me?"

Eduardo looked him in the eye. "Because my life could have easily turned out just like yours. I was headed into a life of crime. Then I met Anna."

She'd saved him. And then nearly destroyed him.

Raul held a twenty-five-kilogram weight but didn't slip it on the bar. "About her. I know it's not my place…"

"You're my friend, Raul. As long as you don't disparage her, say what you want." Eduardo picked up the other twenty-five-kilogram disc, ready to slip it onto the other end of the weightlifting bar. At least he could spot for his friend.

Raul's eyes were wide. "I'd never say anything bad about her. She's so wonderful with Timo, and kind to me too. She insisted I call her Anna. Anyway, I was thinking… You have history with her." Raul held up his hand as Eduardo opened his mouth again. "I don't want to know what happened, but can I give you some advice?"

"If you feel you need to." *Dios*. Everyone was a relationship expert these days.

"When you look at her, all you're remembering is the bad stuff, the way it ended. You just told me she saved you. Look at the good stuff, how you felt when you were together, how she made you a better man. I hated my ex after she left. But without her, I wouldn't have Timo. And he's everything to me. So, yeah, maybe I don't hate her completely. Just … give Anna a chance."

Eduardo had felt amazing when Anna had been in his life. Since then, he'd achieved great success. But he'd never been as happy.

Raul had a point.

Chapter Nine

Anna cradled the warm mug of coffee in her hands. Eduardo sat across from her, spreading jam on a scone. He'd already consumed all the *tostadas*, and this was his third scone. Then again, he had missed dinner last night. Or he'd worked up an appetite in the gym. His long sleep had done wonders as well. He not only looked healthier, but he also seemed more at peace with himself and her— more like the Eduardo she used to know.

"What do you want to know about my mother?" she asked.

His gaze flickered to hers, and for once there was a softness in his eyes when they roamed her face. Had their passionate encounter in the hallway actually burned away some of his animosity?

"Have you talked to her recently?"

"No. I sent her several messages when Abuela died, but she didn't respond. We're … not on speaking terms right now. We had a huge fight when I told her I was getting married." The hate-filled conversation still played back in Anna's mind whenever she was tempted to heal the breach with her only living relative.

"She didn't like Simon?"

"She liked him just fine when he was my music manager."

"Maybe she was worried about the age difference between you?"

"No, I asked. According to her I was 'an ungrateful bitch who was trying to cut her off now that I was finally proving useful in life.' Basically, she knew if I married Simon she'd no longer control my life or career. She wanted to be the one to make decisions about what I wore, where I ate, who I was seen with, that sort of thing. I wanted to grow as an artist and a person. I told her I wanted her to be my mother, my personal support, not my caretaker. Evidently, that wasn't enough for her. So now I pay her forty grand a month to stay out of my life."

"Did she know Simon was dying when you wed?"

"No. We told no one. And I didn't want her to think that once Simon passed she'd be back in charge of me."

He nodded. "You haven't heard from her at all since your engagement was announced?"

"No. She didn't come to the wedding or the funeral, or … anything." He reached across and pulled her fingers from the *factura* she'd been shredding. "Anna, there's no easy way to say this. Is your mother the main beneficiary in your will?"

She clutched his fingers before he could withdraw them. "You think she's behind these incidents?" A chill swept through her. Could her mother hate her so much she wanted her dead?

"It's just one line of inquiry we're investigating. We need to look at everyone's motives. What would she gain if you were … killed?" The last word seemed hard for him to even say.

"She'd get about ten percent of my estate. The rest

goes to various charities. I made a new will after I married Simon, but I felt I had to leave her something. Why, I don't know. Sentimentality, I guess." She took a long sip of her coffee, hoping the warm liquid would dissolve the lump she could feel forming in her throat.

"Ten percent is still a large sum," Eduardo said, almost to himself. "About fifteen million?"

"Something like that. I don't actually keep tabs on how much I'm worth. I have an accounting firm that does that."

"Anna, you shouldn't just blindly trust people."

She picked a few flakes of pastry off the bright maxi-dress she wore. "I know." The only person she could truly trust now sat across from her. "What about my stepfather? I've only met him twice. Maybe he's put her up to this."

"According to my sources, your mother and her husband are no longer together. He moved out of the marital home eight months ago and is living in Florida. He's not under suspicion right now. Should he be?"

Anna pictured the slightly balding, golf-obsessed man her mother had surprisingly introduced as her stepfather the week before Anna had announced her engagement. "I doubt it. He seemed like a nice enough guy. But I had no idea my mother's marriage was in trouble. Maybe that's why she hasn't contacted me. I'll try to call her again this afternoon."

"Remember, don't tell her where you are."

"I won't."

His fingers tightened on hers, just enough to prepare her for his next words. "Also, be prepared for a request for money. I'm told she's amassed huge debts."

Mierda. When they'd lived in Boca, $40,000 US a *year* would have kept all three of them fed, clothed, and sheltered. How could her mother go through that monthly? Anna rarely spent that much, and she had a diva image to live up to. "I won't promise her anything until I know what's happening."

He nodded and went back to devouring his breakfast.

"How did you do it?" she asked after a long silence.

His gaze swung back to hers, his dark eyes troubled. "Do what?"

"Cope, after your papa and abuela died? I know you were never close to them. Obviously, I can't rely on my mother. I feel like I'm in a rowboat in the middle of the ocean. It's calm seas now, but there are clouds gathering on the horizon. Abuela was always my harbor. Even when I was abroad, she was just a phone call or videoconference away. I'm not sure how I'm going to face things without her in my corner."

That got him out of his chair to pull her into his arms.

"It's still raw and new, Anna. Give yourself time. You'll find your anchor. And you have great inner strength; I know that. As for losing my father and grandmother, their passings were a relief, as bad as that sounds. Neither were happy in life. I hope they've finally found peace."

She couldn't be positive, but she was pretty sure his lips grazed the top of her head. It wasn't quite the kiss she wanted, but it would do for now.

"Do you ever think of your mother? Wonder what she's doing now?"

"No." There was a sharp edge to his voice although the hand running up and down her back remained gentle. "When I was really little, I used to dream of her coming back for me and taking me somewhere nice, somewhere like this. By the time I was eleven I hated her and swore that if she did return, I wouldn't even speak to her."

"Has she tried to contact you now that you're Buenos Aires's most eligible bachelor?"

He leaned back, and a little snort-laugh escaped her. His cheeks were flushed. Raul was right—it was fun to tease Eduardo about the unwanted title. His eyes soon turned serious, though.

"She's dead. I googled her name after a fight with my papa when I was a fourteen. According to a newspaper report, she died of a drug overdose on a yacht about eighteen months after she left. I also found her death certificate among my father's papers after he passed."

"All those years and your father never told you your mother was dead?"

"No. What was the point? She was gone either way."

"Do you think that if she hadn't died, maybe she would have come back for you?"

He hauled in a deep breath, his chest expanding against her, pushing her farther away. She was careful not to touch his back but tightened her arms around his waist. "I was part of the life she didn't want. She chose to leave me."

As did you. The unspoken words sliced through her. Could they ever recover from her earlier desertion? Should she even keep trying? Her body, still pressed against his, shouted a resounding *yes*. Her heart, mind, and soul were a little more cautious.

His warmth, his strength, soothed some of her inner turmoil. She searched for a way to keep the conversation going, to keep hold of him for just a few minutes more. "When I give concerts in Scandinavia, I often wonder if my father is in the audience, maybe with his teen daughter, thinking I look vaguely familiar."

"No one has tried to contact you, claiming you're his child? Damn, that's one avenue we haven't checked."

"Lots of men have written saying they're my father. But I've never responded. My team doesn't even show me the correspondence anymore. A true father is someone who kisses their child good night and lifts them up after they've fallen. Whoever supplied the sperm to form me isn't really my dad."

"I agree. But now that you feel all alone, you don't want to see if you can find him?"

"Not really. I'd always wonder if he'd only claim me because of my fame. Do you think that says something about me? Am I selfish?"

"You are never selfish for wanting to be loved for who you are, not what you have."

Said by a man who'd only ever had love briefly. From her.

***

"I feel like one of the servants in *Downton Abbey* waiting for the earl and countess to return from a trip," Anna said. "Except we're standing in the foyer and not outside."

Eduardo's raised eyebrows asked if she'd been drinking, but his mouth said, "*Downton Abbey*?"

Now it was her turn to wonder what planet he lived on. "Don't tell me you've never heard of it."

"Okay, I won't. Even though I haven't."

"I know what we're doing next rainy day—a *Downton Abbey* marathon."

His reply was a sexy smile that kick-started her ovaries. "If it involves you, me, a sofa, a soft blanket, and relative darkness, I'm in. Until then, what would these *Downton Abbey* servants be doing while waiting for their lord and lady to return? Please say they'd be kissing."

"Unlikely, but maybe surreptitiously holding hands. And definitely gossiping."

She slipped her palm into his. It was slightly ridiculous, waiting here for the homeowners to return. But when the guard had called up from the gate to say they were on their way, both she and Eduardo had naturally gravitated towards the front door, ready to greet them when they arrived.

"There's nothing to gossip about. Tiago is married to Vivi, and they adopted his niece Miranda following the death of her parents." There was a little more to the story than that, as she already knew from the cook, who did like to talk. "Accompanying them are Jacques and Maya. Jacques and Tiago have a half brother in common but no other blood tie. But they're both keen vintners so have bonded over that. I'm sure you'll get along with Vivi and Maya. Vivi loves children and is very sweet. Don't get on her bad side, though. Tiago told me she took down a grown man with one kick.

"Maya is… I guess the best way to describe her is 'a force of nature.' But she's very friendly. There was some trouble in the early part of her and Jacques's relationship. That's all behind them now, and they're expecting twins."

Anna tightened her grip on Eduardo's hand and commanded her feet to stay still. Her heels had clicked like a ticking bomb against the marble tiles in the foyer when she'd paced the space earlier. She tried to call on her inner diva, but ever since her realization that she no longer wanted to be Angel exclusively, her alter ego had deserted her. At least she hadn't taken her muse with her and, Anna had written three songs in the days since *The Kiss*. She was finally back in the groove. With her goal of getting her life back on track, she'd set herself a schedule of vocal exercises, stretching, light cardio, and dedicated songwriting.

But she made sure to add in playtime with Timo and long, decadent dinners with Eduardo. They chatted about little things, people they'd known in the past, amusing things Timo had said or done, basically everything and nothing. Eduardo was right: those discussions were the conversational equivalent of a hug.

He had also lived up to his promise to give her the boyfriend experience. He'd been attentive, held her hand, and gently kissed her good night each evening.

He'd sat with her, talked with her, teased her, and made her laugh. He was everything he'd been as her teenage boyfriend, still constrained by his promise to her grandmother.

But she wanted more now. She'd tasted the passion he could ignite in her. She wasn't content with platonic. She wanted him. Every single scorching bit of him. Preferably naked.

The doctor had come this morning and removed the bandages on Eduardo's back. It was healing nicely, but still he cautioned him to take care and not engage in strenuous activity for at least a week more. Did making love count as strenuous? Because she wasn't sure she had a week of restraint left in her. Even standing next to him in the foyer, she wanted to rip off his clothes and fully experience the passion he stirred in her. She shifted, clenching her thighs together as The Kiss replayed in her mind.

"Did you speak with Valentina?" Eduardo asked.

Dios. Mentioning her mother was the most effective contraceptive ever.

Could her parent really be behind the incidents? It seemed impossible. But then she had a hard time believing Valentina could blow forty grand a month. The house and cars were paid for. What was she spending the money on? Did she have a gambling addiction?

"I called several times, but she didn't answer."

He released her hand and wrapped his arm around her shoulder, sheltering her in his embrace. She leaned into his strength for a moment. Soon she'd have to make some tough decisions—about continuing to pay her mother, next steps in her career, finding an anchor in her life…

Next week. She was giving herself a few more days to enjoy being with Eduardo: no strings attached, no commitments. No heartache on the horizon.

Unfortunately, she'd also be with five other people. Seven if she counted Raul and Timo. "This feels so weird, welcoming people into their own home."

Before he could reply, the room was full. There were enough photos of Tiago, Vivi, and Miranda around the house that she recognized them immediately. The very tall man and his heavily pregnant and radiant wife had to be Jacques and Maya. But the little boy who accompanied them was a bit of a mystery. Eduardo had made no mention of another child.

"It's Angel!" Miranda, the young girl, screamed. "*Tio* Eduardo, you never told me you knew Angel! You're holding hands. Are you going to marry her? Can I be your flower girl? I'm going to be flower girl when Tio Daniel marries Max's mother. So I'll have experience." She paused for a tiny breath. "Unless you get married first and then it will be the other way around, I guess."

Eduardo released Anna's hand and kneeled. "You are running ahead of yourself, *pequeña*. This is my friend Anna, and we're not getting married."

Miranda gazed up at Anna, her face scrunched. "She sure looks like Angel."

"When I sing, I use the name Angel. However, my real name is Anna. But I like to keep that a secret. Can you do that for me?"

Miranda crossed her arms and pitched her head to one side. "I will if you sing 'Broken Dreams' for me."

Tiago approached and put a hand on Miranda's shoulder. "Please excuse my niece. She's a born negotiator. I'm Santiago Alvarez, Tiago to my friends. I hope you will consider me as one." He held out a hand to a platinum-blonde woman wearing a black skirt and pink top. "And this is my wife, Genevieve, or Vivi for short."

Vivi held out her hand. "It is lovely to meet you, Anna. I hope Eduardo told you that you are welcome to stay here as long as necessary."

"Thank you. And if it's okay with Miranda, I would like to try out a few of my new songs. Perhaps we could have a mini concert after dinner?"

Miranda bounced up and down. "Max, did you hear that? Angel is going to give us a private concert."

The little boy moved closer, looking unimpressed. "Are any of your new songs about cars?"

Wow, tough audience.

With a laugh, the woman with amazing auburn hair and a belly bump large enough to house a football team ruffled his hair. "This is Max, and he's obsessed with cars. He's our nephew, or will be as soon as Jacques's brother Daniel marries Max's mother. They're in China for the Formula 1 race, so we brought Max with us. I'm Maya, by the way. And a huge fan."

Her husband stepped forward, and Anna resisted the temptation to step back. His face was stern and his size intimidating. "Hello, Anna. *Enchanté*. You've undoubtedly worked out that I'm Jacques." He turned to his wife and his expression softened instantly, prompting Anna to reevaluate her first impression. "Maya, you promised to rest as soon as we got here."

Maya laughed again and put a hand on her husband's cheek. "I will. Just give me a minute." She turned back to Anna. "This is my first pregnancy, and Jacques is a little bit overprotective. Next time I'm not going to tell him I'm expecting until the sixth month, so I only have to endure three months of his constant worrying."

"Keep defying me and there will be no next time," Jacques grumbled.

"Oh, darling, you know you can't resist me," Maya replied. "And I told you, I want six children. Look on the bright side—if we keep doing it in duplicate, that's only two more pregnancies."

"I have to live through this one first." Without giving her a chance to reply, he scooped his wife up in his arms as though she weighed nothing. "Are we in the same room we used last time, Tiago?"

Vivi rushed forward. "Yes, of course. Do you remember where it is, or shall I lead the way?"

"I remember. See you all at dinner," Jacques called out, already making his way to the stairs. "Max, be good and listen to Vivi."

"Sorry for the Neanderthal display," Maya said from halfway up the stairs. "We'll chat later, Anna." There was so much love in her voice it was evident she wasn't upset with her husband.

Tiago put a hand on his wife's waist and drew her closer to his side. "A *nap* sounds like a good idea. It was a long flight. Do you think maybe you should rest, too, Vivi?"

"What? You're expecting already?" Eduardo asked.

Vivi blushed. "No. Not yet."

"But I, too, am unable to resist my wife. Shall I carry you upstairs as well to prove I can?"

"I can walk. Besides, we have guests. We can't disappear the second we walk through the door. And who's going to look after Miranda and Max?" Vivi reminded her husband. "They slept most of the way. I doubt you'll get them to go to bed."

"Don't stay up on my account," Anna said. "We can get to know each other properly later. And I'd love to look after the children." Seeing the other couples interact and the happiness on their faces sent a flutter through her own chest. Would she ever have that? To keep her mind off all she didn't have, she concentrated on what she did. The ability to make people happy with her talent. "Maybe Max could help me write a song about cars?"

"Now you've done it," Miranda said, throwing her hands in the air with such drama Anna had to bite the inside of her cheek to stop a laugh. "Once he starts talking about cars, he never shuts up."

Max's bottom lip began to quiver. Anna kneeled so she could see his eyes. "Well, I know nothing about cars. So I'm glad Max is an expert." She was rewarded with a smile from the little boy. "Perhaps, Miranda, you can help with rhyming words," Anna added, not wanting to diminish her role in their lyrical enterprise.

"I can. I'm very good at rhymes."

"Are you sure you don't mind?" Vivi asked.

Anna gazed at the children's excited faces and felt brighter herself. "I'm sure. Enjoy your rest. We'll see you at dinner." She took both children's hands. "Let's go find my friend Timo to help us. He doesn't speak English, though. Max, do you speak Spanish?"

Max shook his head, but Miranda answered, "I can rhyme and translate."

"You're very good at solving problems, Miranda," Anna said. If only the little girl could tell Anna what to do about her increasing need for Eduardo. But there were some things you couldn't ask an eight-year-old.

Her eyes followed the direction of her thoughts.

Wait. Was that love and longing in Eduardo's expression?

***

Eduardo couldn't take his eyes from Anna as she left with Miranda and Max on their way to find Timo.

"When you're done staring like a lovesick puppy at the woman who is 'just a friend you're not marrying,' perhaps we could discuss business?" Tiago said, a teasing note in his voice. After all the ribbing Eduardo had given his friend when Tiago had fallen in love with Vivi, it was fair enough. Except this wasn't love. Not the reciprocal kind, anyway.

"I never said she was *just* a friend." He also didn't want to discuss it. Because he wasn't sure where he stood with Anna. Their relationship currently oscillated between that of platonic friends and wary exes. Since the hallway encounter, he'd kept a very tight lid on his passion and never allowed himself more than a kiss on the cheek when they said good night. Still, every time she was near, he teetered on the edge of sanity. The doctor's quasi all-clear this morning had been a godsend. He could finally make good on his promise.

But now they had a house full of people. And he really didn't want the inquisition that would inevitably follow if they both disappeared for a day.

Business. He needed to focus on business and not the woman who was driving him insane. Every day she became more and more like the Anna he used to know and less like the international singing sensation the world recognized as Angel. She dressed differently now, because her clothes were purchased by one of the staff, but more often than not, her hair was in a high ponytail rather than the restrained knot at the base of her neck that was Angel's signature hairstyle. She no longer picked at her food but ate with gusto, even stealing some of his dessert when she thought he wasn't paying attention.

He was always paying attention.

A child's squeal of delight, followed by Anna's light laughter, echoed through the house. Something inside him tightened.

"You still with me?" Tiago asked.

"Yeah. But I thought you were going to join your wife?"

"In a bit. She really does need to rest. And she won't if I'm there."

"Then let's go up to your office. I hope you don't mind—I made myself at home over the past few days." They both started up the stairs. "We need to discuss next steps on the community center project. I've arranged a conference call on Tuesday morning with the head of the municipal planning department and the chair of the protest committee. I'm hoping that we may be able to come to some sort of compromise. Where do you suggest we give way? I'm still of the opinion that putting any kind of youth program in our new building will be detrimental to the commercial elements. Could we afford to fund a replacement center somewhere else?"

"Not if we have to purchase land and build it. Maybe we could retrofit an existing building," Tiago said.

"What about a sponsorship?" Anna asked. They both turned and waited for her to catch up to them on the stairs. "Sorry, I didn't mean to eavesdrop or interrupt. It's just that part of Simon's foundation's mandate is to foster music programs in economically deprived areas. We could align our needs and find a suitable location in La Boca. If your company sponsored, say, online gaming tournaments or coding programs to make games and apps, something kids are interested in doing, then it would be a double draw—and a possible charitable write-off."

Tiago's mouth dropped open. "Intriguing idea."

"Think about it. If it works for you, we can present a united front to the planners and protesters alike. Johanna, who is head of the opposition party, is the daughter of one of my grandmother's friends. I'm sure she'd agree. Her son turned to drugs and gangs because he had nothing to do after school, so it's an emotional topic for her." A stray strand of hair caressed her cheek as she talked, and Eduardo had to fist his hand to stop from tucking it behind her ear. "Oh, and in case you think I've abandoned the children already, they're having a snack in the kitchen under the cook's indulgent eye. Timo was helping her bake cookies. I've just come to get my guitar. Evidently, I'm going to write a song about something called a boo-cat-ee."

Tiago laughed. "Bugatti. It's Max's current favorite car. Be glad he's moved on from the Koenigsegg. It's much harder to rhyme."

Anna's answering laugh washed over Eduardo, flooding his soul with peace. He'd never noticed how much tension he carried around with him until it disappeared whenever Anna laughed.

"I like her," Tiago said, after the study door was shut behind them. "As a pop star, I assumed that she'd be stuck-up and narcissistic. But she seemed to genuinely want to spend time with the children. And her idea to appease the protest committee is pure gold. If we go halves on rent and refit with her foundation, then it would be doable. What do you think?"

"It's a brilliant solution." But would it keep him in contact with Anna once she left? He didn't know if that was so good an idea.

The discussion turned to a revised schedule for construction on the basis that they were able to secure planning permission within the next eight weeks. Other projects then were considered, and it wasn't until his stomach growled loudly that Eduardo glanced at his watch. It was nearly three o'clock.

"I didn't realize how late it was," Tiago said. "I'm

just going to check on Vivi, then relieve Anna of childcare duties. I'm sure they've driven her crazy already. Max is a wonderful boy, but he has the energy of a thousand suns."

Eduardo got to his feet, stretching his back muscles carefully. "Are you really considering fatherhood? I remember a time when you wanted to go through life alone."

A rueful grin lifted Tiago's lips. "Vivi is adamant she wants a baby or three. And I must admit, the thought of her having my child is … monumental. As if of all that I might accomplish in life, this would be my greatest achievement, terrifying and exhilarating at the same time. I'll admit, this marriage business is satisfying. You should try it. You're clearly smitten with Anna. I've never seen you like this over a woman."

Eduardo ignored that comment, since it was too near his thoughts to manage a flippant reply. Instead he said, "I'll take childcare duty now. You can have some alone time with Vivi—get started on that greatest achievement."

"I won't say no to that," Tiago replied. With a clap on Eduardo's back, which stung, he went to join his wife.

Eduardo found Anna and the children in the garden. Anna sat on a blanket, her guitar on her lap, a pad of music sheets beside her. Miranda and the two younger boys danced while Anna sang a silly song about a car that said "boo" and scared all the other vehicles away. As she got to the chorus, the children joined her in singing. Even little Timo, who probably didn't understand what he was saying in English, sang as loudly as he could.

A vice clamped around Eduardo's heart and squeezed. Dios, he so wanted this—this domesticity. With her. But he had no idea how to accomplish that. Could he give up his life? What about the promises he'd made to Tiago to take over the day-to-day running of Alva-Suarez? He couldn't pay back years of loyal support, not to mention unwavering friendship, by abandoning him. Plus, he still had Raul's custody case to wrap up.

No, his life was firmly rooted in Argentina. He couldn't just up and leave. Anna had become his whisky—a temptation he had to imbibe in moderation or risk losing everything he'd worked so hard to achieve.

But neither could he ask her to give up her career. She'd put her everything into it for the past ten years. He could see the pleasure she still got from music, even in singing a silly song with the kids. He had no right to take that away from her.

And what of the danger that still followed them? The investigators hadn't been able to uncover anything further. There'd been no mysterious payments or withdrawals made by any of their suspects that would indicate a hired perpetrator. It was a cat-and-mouse game now. Should he and Anna go back to BA and wait for their nemesis to pounce again? Given the escalation in actions, the next one might be deadly. He would not risk her life. But neither could they remain in hiding here forever. Although a little voice in his head asked, "Why not?" As far as lifestyles went, this one was pretty idyllic.

The song came to an end, and Anna raised her gaze from the children to meet his eyes. The radiance and joy on her face pulled an answering smile from him. She looked so happy. The 'why not' voice got louder.

"That song is amazing," he said. "It's sure to be a chart-topper."

She put down her guitar, rose elegantly to her feet, and strolled over to him. "Wait until you hear the one about the Porsche that thinks it's better than everyone else, and then a Mercedes comes along and *smokes it*." She put finger quotes around the last two words. Her eyes sparkled with laughter, her skin glowed from fresh air and sunshine, and her full lips enticed him to taste her sweetness.

"I so want to kiss you right now," he said, sotto voce so the children, who were now playing a game of tag, didn't hear.

"I so want to be kissed by you right now," she replied. Anna placed her hand on his chest and slid it up to his shoulder. Before their mouths could connect, Miranda stood beside them and tugged on his shirt.

"I thought you weren't going to get married. You sure look like you want to get married. Hey, Tio Eduardo, if you married Anna, would that make her my *tia*? How cool would that be? Except could I tell my friends at the park that Angel is my aunt? Or would I have to keep that a secret too?"

Anna dropped her forehead to his shoulder and started to laugh. "I don't think I could ever say that many words without taking a breath." She made no comment on the substance of Miranda's statement.

Eduardo held back a sigh. "Miranda, you are a terrible matchmaker. You have to let the adults sort themselves out. Now, on to more important things. Did you bring me anything from France? I seem to recall you promised me a chocolate croissant."

"I did pack a chocolate croissant for you. Did you know the French people call them *pain au chocolat*, but there's no pain at all? Unless you eat too many, which I did once. Anyway, on the plane ride here, Max's aunt Maya got hungry, and they're her favorites. And then Max got hungry, and basically they all got eaten before we landed. But I'll be sure to bring you some when we go back for Tio Daniel's wedding."

Anyone who heard her now would never believe that following the tragic death of her parents, Miranda had been mute until Vivi had worked her child-caring magic.

While Miranda was spinning her sad tale of the demise of his chocolate croissants, Anna moved out of his arms and picked up her guitar once more. Another echo from the past slammed into him. She'd rarely been without her guitar when they'd dated as teens. How many times had he kissed her with the stupid thing on her back, hindering his attempts to unhook her bra?

"Where are my backup dancers?" she called. "Let's put on a rehearsal so we're ready for our big show tonight. Eduardo, you can be our audience."

She tossed the blanket at him, and the three children organized themselves around her with Timo, the smallest, in front and Max and Miranda on either side.

Anna strummed her guitar a few times, and the children swayed their hips from side to side. Timo kept his eyes on Miranda so he could follow her lead. Then Anna started to sing. Her voice, strong and smooth, even made the silly song sound ethereal.

He tried to keep his eyes off her and concentrate on the children and their movements, which were downright hysterical. Miranda had obviously been in charge of choreography. Princess twirls and curtsies formed the backbone of the routine, not really in keeping with a ditty about cars.

The third song left the vehicular sphere and entered the world of heartbreak. The boys sat down but Miranda kept dancing, her little body swaying with the haunting melody. Each pick of the guitar strings felt like she was plucking the notes from his heart.

"This is my latest," Anna said, not quite meeting his eyes. "I'm calling it 'Afraid to Love Again.'"

I stand here on a precipice
Two choices for me remain
To love you or to walk away
Can I bear to do this again?

But then, oh, I remember the joy
Of being in your arms
And oh God, I can't deny
I'm so tempted by you, boy

I'm afraid to love you again

Dare I gamble my heart anew?
'Cause this time I know if we break
My heart will never recover
More than that … what scares me the most
Am I even enough for you now?

You dangle love before my eyes
Make me wish for all that we had
But it took me years to even repair
A heart that was hurt so bad

But then, oh, I remember the bliss
Of the way you held me so close
And oh God, I can't deny
I am longing for your kiss

I'm afraid to love you again
Dare I gamble my heart anew?
'Cause this time I know if we break
My heart will never recover
More than that … what scares me the most
Am I even enough for you now?

So here I stand before you
Wanting so hard to believe
That everything we once gave up
We could again achieve

But then, oh, I remember the pull
To spend each day with you
And oh God, I can't deny

How you made my life so full

I'm afraid to love you again
Dare I gamble my heart anew?
'Cause this time I know if we break
My heart will never recover

More than that ... what scares me the most
Am I even enough for you now?

More than that ... what scares me the most
Am I even enough for you now?

He ached to pull Anna into his arms and reassure her of his love.

And if that didn't prove how much of a fool he was, he didn't know what would.

Chapter Ten

Anna's heart beat furiously as the last chords of her newest song hung in the air.

Her eyes met his over the top of Miranda's head as the little girl dozed in Eduardo's lap having stopped dancing before the start of the last song. The two boys had likewise fallen asleep on the blanket beside him.

"Is it too late?" she asked, her voice raw, but not from singing.

He didn't pretend to misunderstand her question. "I don't know. I can't see a way forward. All we may have is here and now." He spoke low. So as not to wake the children? Or was his throat clogged with longing as well?

"I'll take the here and now. And work towards a future." There, she'd said it. She was willing to risk her heart again. Was he?

He nodded his head at the children. "We'll talk more tonight."

She swung her guitar to her back and kneeled next to Eduardo. She intended to pick up a sleeping Timo and carry him inside. Instead, she drowned in the depths of Eduardo's eyes. "Only talk?"

A fire blazed in the chocolaty richness, but his words were steady. "We'll also talk about not just talking."

Eduardo glanced to the right and she followed his gaze. Tiago and Vivi approached, arm in arm.

"Well done, Anna. You got them all to sleep," Tiago said. "If the singing thing doesn't work out for you, consider a career in child care."

"I may have to do that," she replied, "if my songs are that boring."

"More likely the long flight and time change are catching up with them," Vivi said.

Tiago took Miranda from Eduardo, who picked up Max. The little boy, whose hair color was so similar to Eduardo's they could be father and son, snuggled into his chest and exhaled a sigh.

Vivi reached for Timo, but Anna put her hand out to stop her. She needed this connection.

"I've got him," Anna said. Timo was a lot heavier asleep than awake, but when he, too, snuggled into her arms, any muscle strain was worth it. This was what she'd given up for her career. It didn't seem worth it. She'd proven herself. She'd been a success. So what if her career was on the wane? Maybe now was the perfect time to find some other joy in life. She could probably get out of her recording contract; other artists did it all the time.

Except then she'd be coming at this life change from a point of weakness, not strength. Eduardo deserved to be more than her backup plan. He had to be her first choice, not her only choice.

Vivi grabbed the blanket and the children's empty juice boxes and followed behind.

"Drinks on the terrace in ten minutes," Tiago said before they all went in different directions to deposit their precious bundles.

Raul raced forward as Anna navigated down the hall towards his room. From the dampness of his clothes, he'd been washing something. As far as she'd seen, the man hadn't sat down once since he'd been here. She halted the gratitude on his lips with a smile.

"No need to thank me. We all love spending time with Timo. He's no trouble. You should be happy so many people want to care for him. We all get a chance to bask in his bubbly personality. Just show me where I can put him down."

Raul opened a door and she strode into the room. A small bed had been placed against a wall in the corner, and she gently laid Timo there.

After pulling the blanket at the base of the bed up over the little guy's shoulders, she dropped a kiss on his forehead. Her breath caught in her throat. Would she ever get to tuck in a child of her own? Dios, she was becoming maudlin. She needed to keep busy. All this domesticity was making her second-guess her decision to put her career first.

Or was it anticipation for tonight with Eduardo that made her restless?

She freshened up and joined the others on the terrace. Jacques and Tiago were drinking red wine, comparing the various notes they could taste.

"Welcome, Anna. What can I get you to drink?" Tiago asked when he spotted her hovering in the doorway.

"Just a glass of water. My throat is dry from singing all afternoon." She accepted the glass and sat on the chair nearest the sofa, where Maya and Vivi lounged. Eduardo was nowhere to be seen.

"I heard your new songs," Maya said. "Jacques and I were sitting on the balcony when you began your rehearsal concert. May I be the first to say they were amazing? I was in tears through all of them. Even the one about the bragging car. I'm such a watering pot these days."

"I was crying too," Vivi added. "Not during the car ones; those made me laugh. But the one about the hurricane heart really touched me. My brother had an addiction to drugs, and although we loved him, he left devastation in his wake. Yet somehow, after listening to your song, I felt better. I know he didn't mean to hurt us, but at the time it was hard to see him self-destruct and not take it as a personal rejection of our love."

And this is why she sang, so others could process their own emotions. "If you all heard me earlier, then there's no need for a concert after dinner."

"Yes, there is," Maya said. "I want to hear them again. We all do. Right, Eduardo?"

"Yes, of course," he answered, although whether he knew what he was agreeing to or not was another question. He'd moved to join the men, but rather than a glass of wine, he, too, held a tumbler of water. He'd changed out of his jeans and polo shirt into black dress pants and a charcoal gray button-down. His dark hair was still damp and a little curly at the back. Her fingers tightened on the glass she held.

Would he make love to her tonight? Or find some excuse to put her off?

He caught her staring and excused himself from the other men to join her. He perched his incredible backside on the side of her chair and put his arm along the back. It wasn't quite an embrace, but it still signaled that they were a couple. Warmth filled her, and she leaned into his side.

"They want me to sing again," she said softly. Vivi and Maya had embarked on a conversation about pregnancy, and Tiago and Jacques were still analyzing wine on the other side of the terrace.

"The children will be disappointed if they don't get to perform before a larger audience," he said at last.

"Provided they wake up."

That faint hope of reprieve died when Miranda arrived a couple of minutes later, rubbing the sleep from her eyes. Max followed in her wake. But unlike the barely awake girl, he bounded onto the terrace like a consummate showman about to begin a performance. He made a beeline for Eduardo.

"Uncle Eduardo, what car do you drive?" Max asked.

"I had a BMW 6 Series Gran Turismo, but it was wrecked last week. I'm in the market for a new vehicle. What do you suggest?"

Max tilted his head and announced, "A Pagani Zonda."

"A Zonda? That's a little out of my league. And not really practical for city driving."

Max shrugged. Practicality was something only

grownups worried about.

"He wants you to get that car because he doesn't know anyone who owns one," Jacques said. "And he's hoping you'll give him a ride."

Jacques and Tiago seemed to have finished their vintner discussion and now joined the rest of them. Jacques's fingers massaged the back of Maya's neck. She leaned into his touch like a cat being stroked. Tiago had, similar to Eduardo, perched on the arm of the chair nearest Vivi, and he caressed her shoulders.

How could she sing of lost love to these people who had it by the bucketload?

"Then you should get a Mercedes," Max said, pulling everyone's attention back to him. "My new daddy drives a Mercedes—a super duper fast one."

Eduardo smiled. "Then it must be the best car ever. I will definitely consider one of those."

The conversation turned away from vehicles to what Miranda had seen in France and what she liked the best. Which basically was the "mega cool house with hundreds of rooms" and Maya's dog Princess, who'd recently had a litter of puppies.

Anna let the conversation swirl around her. It was nice not to be the center of attention. She spent most of her time in LA being fawned over while she attempted to stay in character. She was an actress in a never-ending role. How had she not seen that until just now?

"Are you okay?" Eduardo whispered into her ear.

She smiled up at him. "I'm getting there."

"I knew you would." His sexy smile warmed her from the inside.

Maya's question, "Anna, when's your next album coming out?" brought her attention back to the rest of the group.

"Soon, I hope. It's already a month late. But my record label has cut me some slack with all that's been happening in my life recently. Which is a good thing, because until a week ago, I had only two new songs written. Lately, though, I've been inspired. So hopefully I'll have something out before the end of the year."

Eduardo stiffened beside her. How ironic that the songs he'd sparked would be what took her away from him again.

That was a problem for another day. As he'd said earlier, they had the here and now. And she was going to enjoy every last second.

***

Eduardo leaned back in his chair. Dinner had been blissfully quick. Miranda had asked earlier if she and Max could eat in the kitchen with Timo so they could go over their dance routine a couple more times. Evidently, she'd had a rethink on the choreography and wanted to teach the boys a couple of new moves.

He had tried to convince Raul and Timo that they were welcome to join the group in the dining room. But his friend had insisted they were more comfortable in the kitchen. And as neither of them spoke English, which was the lingua franca now that Jacques and Maya had arrived, it would make it awkward for someone to have to translate conversations so they could feel included.

So it was just the adults. But for a reason no one wanted to explain, they were anxious to rejoin the children rather than revel in their ability to eat dinner without having to cut someone's meat or remind someone to eat their green beans.

They chatted about the next day's activities. Jacques and Tiago were heading off to see Jacques's vineyard in Chile but would be back before evening. Maya and Vivi planned to spend the time relaxing by the pool.

Anna fidgeted in her seat beside him.

He leaned close, taking a moment to inhale her spicy vanilla scent. "You don't have to perform if you don't want. Say your throat is sore."

She smiled at him. "No, it's okay. As you said, the children will be disappointed. Ignore me. I'm always like this before a performance."

"You never used to be. You loved an audience. That was one of the things that made you great. People could tell you genuinely wanted to sing for them."

"I still do. It's just there are so many more expectations of me these days. It's hard to live up to the ideal with every performance."

"Well, you don't have to worry about that with this group. Just be yourself. Be Anna. Besides, most eyes will be on the kids dancing."

"If you say so. Still…" She stood, not waiting for the dessert course. "If you will all please excuse me, I'd like to prepare."

"Yes, of course," Maya replied. "If it's too much—"

"No. I'd like to sing for you and get some audience

reaction to my new songs."

"See you in a bit, then," Vivi said.

He caught Anna's hand as she pushed in her chair. "Do you need any help?"

Finally, a genuine smile. "No. I can dress myself. I won't be long."

It was odd how those few minutes felt like an eternity. He gazed around the table at the other couples. The love in the room was thick enough to choke a hippopotamus. A trickle of unease crept down his spine. This time next year, would he still be on the outside looking in, envying the others' loving families?

Maya was the next to excuse herself, saying her bladder was being used as a bouncy castle. Vivi departed as well, so it was just the three men and the last dregs of their dinner wine.

Tiago cleared his throat. "You'll regret it if you let her get away, Eduardo."

Except his friend didn't know she'd already gotten away once. And how hard Eduardo had regretted that. Could he sacrifice what it would take to keep Anna in his life permanently? He wouldn't be the only one to pay the price. Tiago had offered him the partnership so he could spend more time with Vivi and Miranda. If Eduardo left to follow Anna around the world…

Jacques shifted awkwardly and added, "I never knew I could wake up each day happier than the one before."

"I'll keep that in mind," Eduardo said.

Tiago grabbed the wine bottle like a lifeline. "Who wants a top-up before we go out and join the others?"

Through the open door they could hear the excited chatter of the children already on the terrace and Raul's deep voice telling them to be careful.

Eduardo declined the drink. He'd need all his self-control to make it through the concert. And then to make a rational decision afterward about how far to take things with Anna.

When they stepped out onto the terrace, he did a double take. While they'd eaten dinner, someone had strung fairy lights into the potted palms and formed a makeshift stage covered with a patterned carpet. Candles set up everywhere flickered in the gentle breeze. The patio furniture had been relocated to form a semicircle around the stage. Behind that, more chairs from various parts of the house were arranged.

"Anna said she didn't mind if the staff listened in," Tiago said.

Great, now the world would know the convoluted state of their personal relationship.

Everyone was there except Anna. They didn't have to wait long, however, as she soon appeared from behind the drawn curtains that formed the background for the stage.

He hoped he wasn't the only one to gasp at her appearance. But his heart beat too loudly to hear the others. She wore a pale blue off-the-shoulder gown. The skirt was layers and layers of filmy material. But when she stepped forward, her leg showed almost to the top of her thigh. Her hair, which she normally wore up, curled lightly and floated about her face and down her back and shoulders. Whatever she'd done to her makeup made her look like she'd been thoroughly ravished and was just waiting for her lover to recover so they could go at it again.

Angel had gone sexy.

She perched herself on the stool set up in the middle of the stage and arranged the dress so she was covered demurely. Her old, battered guitar was incongruous with the rest of her ensemble.

"Anna, before you start," Maya said, "do you mind if I record the children dancing? I'd like to send the video to Max's mother."

"That's fine. As long as it goes no further than that. Please ask her not to share. My record label will have a fit if a new song, even one about cars, leaks before release."

A laptop had been set up on a chair beside her, and she pressed a few keys. A quirky background beat filled the air. She nodded to the children. They took up their positions as they had for the rehearsal earlier in the day. Except this time as Anna sang about the cars, Miranda twirled and the boys pretended to be driving around, fake steering wildly to avoid each other and Miranda.

All the adults wore huge smiles. Vivi and Maya had happy tears streaming down their faces. Jacques took the phone from his wife's hand to finish the recording while he put a loving arm around her shoulders. Even Raul seemed to be sniffling suspiciously.

After the second song, Anna called a little intermission. Max climbed onto his soon-to-be uncle's lap. Timo made his way to his father, who picked him up and hugged him close, pressing dozens of kisses on the smiling child's face. Anna handed Miranda a length of white diaphanous material.

"These next two songs I wrote shortly before my husband died. But don't worry, they're not as morbid as that sounds."

Eduardo steeled himself to hear her sing of her love for another man. His throat tightened as she sang of thankfulness for the time they'd shared and admiration for a life well lived. But instead of the jealousy he expected, he was filled with a sense of amazement that she'd found meaning and peace during a turbulent time in her life.

During the song, Miranda fluttered around the stage, using the fabric Anna had given her at times like a sail, at times like a blanket.

"You look just like your mother when you dance, *preciosa*," Tiago said when she sat down in his lap after the second song ended.

Anna shifted on the stool, letting her dress fall to the side, revealing one long leg. She adjusted her hair so it cascaded down one side. One curl slipped into her cleavage. Eduardo wriggled in his seat, trying to find a comfortable spot while his hands clenched the armrests.

She began the next song without the guitar. He'd heard 'Memory Palace' before, but it was just as devastating the second time, further eroding the walls he'd built around his heart to keep him from being vulnerable to anyone again.

"I'm seeing you in an entirely different light now," Tiago whispered as Anna prepared for the next song. Vivi jabbed him in the ribs with her elbow before he could say anything else.

"My next song is called 'Hurricane Heart.'"

She stood, put down the guitar, and just sang. No instrument masked the power and beauty of her voice. Each note pulled another drop of emotion from those listening.

As I leave, I look back over my shoulder
At what I've left behind
Not a single thing is standing
Devastation is all I find

My heart is like a hurricane
Leaving destruction in its wake
I never meant to hurt you
Or make your whole soul ache

I blew in a springtime zephyr
I left a category seven
Your love, you know, it strengthened me
It gave me a glimpse of heaven

The injuries you sustained
They're really not that rare
I burn all bridges after me
To anyone brave enough to care

My heart is like a hurricane
Leaving destruction in its wake
I never meant to hurt you

Or make your whole soul ache

Your eyes they once shone with love
Your smile would make my day
Then my hurricane heart took over
Now all that's left is dead and gray

Our love it once blossomed
Tended carefully by you
Now that field, it has been napalmed
The ashes soaked with dew

My heart is like a hurricane
Leaving destruction in its wake
I never meant to hurt you
Or make your whole soul ache

Never love a hurricane
It's really not that wise
Destruction is our calling card
Leaving a tear that never dries

When the echo of the last note faded into the night, everyone sat stunned.

"*Dios mío*," one of the housekeepers said in a reverential whisper. It broke the spell Anna's amazing voice cast, and the applause was almost as long as the last song.

She accepted it with good grace, although he could see that she'd reverted to her alter ego. Angel had taken over once again.

Tiago glanced over at Eduardo then announced, "Right, the show's over."

Everyone stood; the staff grabbed their chairs and disappeared. Jacques had a sleepy Max on one shoulder while he led a sobbing Maya away with an arm around her waist. "Damn pregnancy hormones," she said as she wiped at her cheeks.

Tiago hoisted up Miranda and held Vivi's hand as they too went inside.

Eduardo was rooted to the spot. He was trapped by his promise to his father to always be his own man and his commitments to Tiago and Raul. Anna had to be free to do what she loved.

All he had left to give her was … pleasure.

Chapter Eleven

Anna picked up the length of fabric Miranda had dropped to give herself a moment. Eduardo hadn't moved when everyone else left. A few of the candles had gutted out during her performance, and she snuffed out a couple on the way over to him.

"Well?" she asked when he finally met her gaze.

"You can never stop singing," he said, his voice husky. "The world needs Angel."

Not what she'd wanted to hear. "What do you need?" She cupped his cheek with one hand while the other rested over his heart. It beat strong and steady beneath her fingers.

Her own pulse raced, partly due to the adrenaline that always carried her through a set.

But mostly because the moment was upon them.

He'd promised her heaven.

And she was here to collect.

Eduardo pulled in a deep breath. "I need you."

Right answer.

"Shall we take this upstairs?" she asked.

"Anna, are you sure this is what you want? We may have feelings for each other and an attraction that's never died. But we're different people now. We can't go back and undo what was done."

"It's not the past I want to undo."

"We don't have a future either. You can't stay. I see the energy, the joy you get from performing. It's not just Angel—it's who you really are. Who you've always been. Angel is just packaging. Anna is the real star. If you try to give that up, you'll miss it like my mother regretted giving up her glamorous modeling life. But I can't follow you, either. I've made promises to Tiago and Raul. I've made promises to myself. I've made plans for my future. As much as I still care for you, I have to be true to who I am as a man."

She stepped back to look him in the eyes without straining her neck.

"After my first two weeks in LA, I wanted to come back to you. Everyone—my mother, my agent, my voice coach, my stylist—told me that our love wouldn't last. Everyone said we were too young, that we'd change, grow apart, fall out of love. Everyone said if I didn't take the opportunity before me, if I didn't do what they—the *experts*—said, I'd live to regret it. Know what? I regret listening to everyone. Dios, Eduardo, each day I regret not waking up next to you. Please, I'm just asking for one day without regret. I know we can't go back. But can't we at least end it differently this time?"

Her eyes searched his, unable to read the conflicting emotions displayed there.

Without a word, he swept her up in his arms and stopped only when they reached his bedroom door. "Promise me one thing?" he said as he set her on her feet in the hallway.

"What's that?"

"Promise that if it's not good the first time, because you overwhelm my senses, you won't sing about it to the world?"

"I promise." She turned the handle and, with a tug on his tie, pulled him into the room with her.

Now that she was here, she wasn't quite sure what to do. Yes, she'd seen movies, read books, overheard play-by-play recaps by some of her dancers who were lovers. But she'd never actually worked out the logistics of this seduction in her mind. She'd always assumed that Eduardo would take the lead and she'd ride the bliss train to orgasmville.

He stood there, his arms at his sides, a sultry smile on his lips. Damn the man. This was his way of making sure he didn't manipulate her into anything she didn't want. Well, news flash: she wanted him. Where were her performance lessons when she really needed them? Should she take off her dress? Wait for him to remove it? Should she start on his clothes? Because she was damn sure all the awkwardness would disappear if he were naked.

A kiss. That seemed the easiest approach. She slid her hands up his rock-hard chest, divesting him of his dinner jacket, then pulled his head down to meet her upturned lips.

She traced his mouth with her tongue, playfully nibbled on his full lower lip. He responded, but not with the passion she knew he was capable of. Was she doing it wrong? Could sex be done wrong?

Unbuttoning his shirt seemed to be the next step after she loosened his tie, so she worked on that while she trailed kisses along his jaw to his ear. He hauled in a deep breath as she sucked his earlobe into her mouth. His hands tightened on her hips, but still he didn't move.

"A little help here? I'm doing all the work," she said as she slipped his shirt off his shoulders. It caught at his wrists because she'd neglected to unbutton the cuffs.

"I'm trying to marshal my self-control," he said, his voice gruff. "I don't want to go all caveman on you. But right this second, all I can think to do is rip that glorious dress from your body and devour every inch of you."

Her skin heated. "A little caveman would be okay. I'll let you know if it gets too rough."

But rather than rip the dress off her, he slid the zipper down inch by exasperating inch, his finger tracing its progress all the way. When it pooled at her feet, he stepped back to admire his handiwork.

"Bra. Off."

She complied without thinking. She went to slip off her silver-heeled sandals, but he stopped her with a shake of his head.

"Leave the shoes on."

"And the panties?" She pulled the lacy fabric away from her hip and his eyes blazed.

"They can stay as well. For now."

Her nipples pebbled under his gaze as he undid his cuffs and tossed his shirt and tie on top of her abandoned dress. Finally, finally, he reached out and caressed her skin. One finger traced the line of her collarbone then dipped between her breasts to tour her navel before making a return journey up.

His other hand joined the party, and both thumbs

and forefingers tugged on her taut nipples. A low moan escaped her lips.

"That's it, *querida*. Tell me what you like, what you want."

"More. Your mouth."

"Here?" he asked as he kissed her shoulder. He lifted her hand to his lips. "Maybe here, on your wrist?"

"Yes, my wrist. That's where I've always wanted to be kissed by you." *Dios*. The man was maddening.

He circled his tongue around the prominent bone on her wrist, and her knees weakened. Was that one of those unknown erogenous zones, or was he just that good? While his mouth was busy there, however, his other hand went exploring.

"Move your legs apart," he whispered while kissing his way up her arm. His mouth was level with her breast; she twisted to connect it with his cheek. A soft chuckle whooshed air over her sensitive skin. But he took the hint and pulled her breast into his mouth with a deep suck while his tongue flicked her nipple.

At the same time, his fingers traced the line of her underwear between her legs. She should have taken them off when she had the chance. Because all her hands were good for was clutching his shoulders to keep upright.

He edged her backward until her spine came up against the post of his bed. "Hold on," he said, guiding her hands to the carved wood above her head. She dug her nails into the timber as he lapped first at one breast then the other. One finger continued to torture her between her legs while he molded and plucked with the other hand at the breast that wasn't currently being flicked into a frenzy of sensation by his tongue and lips.

Liquid fire flowed through her veins, threatening to melt her knees and bring her to the ground.

"How come you still have most of your clothes on?" she asked when she could draw enough breath into her lungs to talk.

"Because this time it's all about you."

Whatever reply she thought to make evaporated from her brain as his finger slipped beneath the fabric and found her nub of pleasure. She clutched the post as wave after wave of ecstasy buffeted her body. When her legs gave way, he wrapped an arm around her waist and held her against him, which really did nothing to help her come down from the sexual high.

"Good?" he asked with a laugh, his lips against her ear.

She forced playfulness into her tone. "Ya know, it was okay. But I'm still missing something." She tried to wedge a hand between them to grasp his manhood, but he caught her questing hand and held it behind her back. "I ache, Eduardo. I want you inside me. What are you going to do about it?"

"Give you a shower." He tossed her over his shoulder, pulling her shoes and panties off as he strode into the adjoining bathroom. "Is this caveman enough for you?"

"There is a perfectly good bed in the other room."

"Ah, but I want to see you wet and soapy. I've had fantasies for days, Anna. All featuring you naked."

He set her on her feet, and she put her hair up with

the few pins in it. He flicked on the water and she walked into the glass-walled shower, standing back until the water warmed a bit. The hot water felt good, but not as good as Eduardo's hands.

"Aren't you joining me?" He leaned against the sink, still wearing his pants. Hell, even his buckle was done up.

"Not yet. Leave the door open. Wash yourself."

"It would be more pleasurable if you washed me."

"I'll dry you off." With that promise, she put on a show of lathering herself with body wash then rinsing it off. She had to admit, being watched was a definite titillation. The sharp, citrusy scent of the soap was in stark contrast to the languid heat that flowed through her veins.

She stepped from the shower to his arms spread wide with a waiting towel. Although it was soft, he dragged the towel over her skin in brisk, efficient movements, so she was pink from head to toe when he was done. Every nerve ending wanted to riot, or at least issue its own complaint, over the indelicate handling.

She glanced at his face. The steely features were impossible to read. She'd expected to see this side of his personality in the courtroom, not the bed or bathroom.

"Go lie down. I'll be with you shortly," he said.

"No."

He tossed the towel on the rack and turned back to her. "Have you had enough? Changed your mind?"

"No. I still want to make love with you. But I want to do it *with* you. I don't want to be treated like a paid companion or someone you picked up in a bar."

His eyes closed for a second and when he opened them again, she saw stark pain. "I didn't know it would be this hard."

Her blood drained to her feet, and the heat she'd felt earlier was replaced with icy tendrils of insecurity. She grabbed another towel and wrapped it around herself. "It's so hard making love to me?"

"It's so hard pretending this is just sex. I can't distance myself from my emotions unless I become domineering."

"Would it be so bad to let your emotions show?"

He raked an unsteady hand through his hair. "You have your songs. You can let your feelings pour out in music and lyrics and the incredible way your voice touches other people's hearts. If I tell you what I feel, it will be a burden to you."

"Why?"

"Because right now I want to imprint your touch, your taste, your very essence into my memory bank and feast on it forever. I want to throw away everything I've worked so hard to achieve just to be with you. And that terrifies me."

The lump in her throat reduced her voice to a whisper. "Why is loving me so scary?"

At last he touched her, this thumb rubbing a gentle caress across her lower lip. "You don't need me, Anna. You have Angel and millions of adoring fans."

"You're wrong." *So, so very wrong.*

He shook his head, a sad smile creasing his lips. "I'm not."

Words weren't going to be enough to convince him.

"Where do we go from here?" She was still standing practically naked in his bathroom, aching with a desire only he could fill. "How about, just like I release my feelings in my songs, you do the same with your touch? Show me what you feel, Eduardo. Make me believe the passion."

"And tomorrow or the day after?"

"They don't exist. We have now. Make it last forever."

His lips replaced his thumb on her mouth, and he kissed her like he'd never stop. Her breath, her heart, her soul deserted her and became one with this man.

The towel fell to the floor and his fingers skimmed over areas they'd touched before. But it was different this time. This time, it meant something.

Just when she thought her legs wouldn't hold her any longer, he lifted her reverently and placed her on the bed as though she were a priceless artwork. He shed his pants and shoes and socks. His boxer briefs were distorted in the front.

As he'd promised days before, he had her writhing beneath him. Her body responded to his every touch. He whispered words of devotion as he kissed every inch of her skin. Her spirit soared within while her heart memorized every minute. This had to last her a lifetime.

Because it was patently obvious. There was no other man for her.

She was floating back down following her second climax when Eduardo suddenly got off the bed.

"Where are you going?" She managed to push herself into a sitting position, but there was no way her legs would carry her across the room to follow him. If he meant to leave her now…

"To get condoms. I forgot to put them in the bedside drawer." He'd shucked his boxers on the way, and for the first time she saw him completely naked. Her body tapped into an energy store she hadn't even known she had.

This had to be special for him as well. "We don't need them."

That halted his progress towards the bathroom. "What do you mean?"

"I'm on the pill. And I've had no other lovers."

He paused. "I've never had sex without protection."

As she'd suspected. "Then it will be a first time for both of us." She rolled onto her knees and held her arms out wide.

"Dios, Anna." He moved back to the side of the bed but didn't climb on. "Are you sure about this?"

"If you ask me that one more time, I'm going to gag you and tie you to the bed."

His deep, sexy chuckle tickled her skin. "Now I don't know whether to ask again or not."

"Get on the bed, Eduardo. Can you lie on your back, or is it too painful?" It was her time to explore.

"It's fine."

"Then it's my turn to taste you."

He piled the pillows against the headboard and relaxed against them. "I want to watch," he said.

She straddled his thighs, and he immediately reached for her breasts again, but she pushed his questing hands back. "Hands behind your head. Like I said, this is my turn."

A frown marred his forehead, but he did as she asked. "I don't want to complain before you've started, but make it quick. I'm so ready for you, I don't think I can last long."

Her body was stirring again as well. And more than anything, she wanted him inside her. But he deserved some payback for earlier. Taking her breasts in each hand, she touched her nipples to his, circling and teasing until that wasn't enough. She lowered her head and flicked his hardened peaks with her tongue as he'd done to her, eliciting a similar response.

She trailed kisses down his stomach while her hands explored. His hip bones were ticklish to her touch, but when she licked them, he moaned. She wanted to spend days touching him, discovering what he liked, what drove him wild. She wanted to claim his body so completely he'd never even look at another woman.

"Two minutes, Anna. You have two more minutes before I take over."

It wasn't going to happen, but spurred on by the warning, she took him in her mouth. Thirty seconds in, he abandoned his laidback posture and sat upright, clutching the sheets with one hand. The other found her clit and worked that into a frenzy. She had to release him from her mouth, because breathing was all she could manage.

He made a move to roll her beneath him, but she resisted. When his eyes met hers, she straddled him once more, positioning them both. As she slid down an inch, a loud moan escaped his lips.

She took him a bit deeper and hit her barrier as he took her mouth in a blistering kiss, one full of passion and promise and … love? His hands tightened on her hips, but she ignored the silent command and plunged down his full length.

Her gasp was caught in his kiss.

"Are you okay?" he asked, his voice tight.

"Amazing," was all she managed to say. There was a sting deep inside, but even that small discomfort faded when she kissed him. He filled her, stretched her, completed her.

His cock twitched within her, and she could tell from his rigid muscles what it took to hold steady while she adjusted.

"Dios, Anna. This is so good," he said. His thumb traced her bottom lip before he lowered his hand to caress her breast.

An urge to move invaded her muscles, and she ground her hips against his before lifting slightly to plunge back down again. He sucked her other nipple into his mouth, and she moved more urgently. Pressure built once more inside, different from when he'd stimulated her with his hands and lips. This was more relentless, demanding movement, demanding fulfillment.

She tossed her head back, put her hand on his shoulders, and rode him like a novice on a runaway horse. She was glad this wasn't being filmed, because there was no finesse to her movements, only need.

"So close," she huffed. Her hair had fallen from her hasty updo and swirled around her, in her face, her mouth.

He flipped her over without withdrawing and drove home their pleasure. She came, screaming his name and inflicting new injuries on his shoulders.

With one final thrust, he went rock hard within her, triggering another wave of molten sensation through her core. He collapsed on top of her, anchoring her to the bed. Didn't matter. She never wanted to move again.

"Edio, *te amo*." The "I love you" slipped from her lips without conscious thought.

He stiffened above her before rolling off.

***

Damn. It sucked to have a pinnacle experience at only thirty years old. The rest of his life loomed long and empty before him. That had been the ultimate sexual encounter. Hell, the ultimate personal one. Being with Anna, making love to her—*with* her—had been even better than he'd imagined.

She was so responsive; his every touch had resulted in a moan of pleasure from her lips. And that was nothing compared to the way she made him feel: like he was her everything. Like he mattered. Only him. She'd chosen him.

It was intoxicating. She undoubtedly felt the same. That's why the "I love you" had fallen from her lips. It was an involuntary reaction to a new experience.

He wrapped an arm around her shoulders and moved her so her head lay against his chest. There was no way he could let her go so soon. Returning her to her own room was not an option. Besides, she'd asked for one morning where she woke without regret.

And he wanted one morning where he woke with her in his arms.

"Sleep now. I'll undoubtedly wake you in a few hours to do that all again. If you're not too sore, that is." He'd never had a virgin in his bed before.

"I've heard that men don't want to talk afterward," she mumbled against his chest. Her hot breath blew across his nipples, stirring to life the cock he'd thought satiated.

"I have no words, Anna." None that he could burden her with. "You told me to express my feelings in my touch. I did that."

"Yes, you did." Another yawn.

He knew the moment she relinquished reality and drifted off to sleep. Her head got heavy over his heart and her hand, which had been gripping his ribcage like she was afraid he'd disappear, loosened its hold.

Carefully, he slid from the bed, tucking the blankets around Anna to keep her warm.

There was no trace of Angel in her appearance. Her hair was a complete mess and would probably take hours to untangle tomorrow. Her lips were swollen from his kisses. There were likely a few red marks on her breasts where his stubble had rubbed against the sensitive skin, not that she'd complained. She looked thoroughly ravished. He rubbed a clenched fist over his clavicle to ease the sudden ache there.

He forced his feet to move towards the bathroom and the beckoning shower. Dios, when Anna had washed herself, he'd nearly come in his pants like a horny teenager. Even now the vision danced before his eyes, making him hard.

He nearly jumped from his skin when a hand connected with his cock and began stroking.

"One thing that has changed in the past ten years," Anna said, "is that I now demand equal opportunity. No one gets to make decisions for me. Such as leaving me to sleep when there are better things to do. And what makes you think you get to shower without an audience?"

"This is more than just watching," he ground out, his teeth clenched as she continued to pump him with her hand. *Mierda*, he was so close to coming again.

"I've always preferred an active role in a performance," she said.

"Anna…"

He tried to formulate words. It was too soon; she'd be too sore. But all he could think was how much he wanted to sink into her hot, wet, tight channel—oh Dios, so tight—and lose the rest of his mind.

"Shh." She put a finger on his lips, and her tongue flicked his nipple for added emphasis. "This night is all about me. And I want this."

She dropped to her knees and once more took him in her mouth while her other hand played with his balls. He locked his legs and leaned against the cool tiles for support. Hot water bounced off his chest and streamed down her face. Her wet hair was plastered to her body. He couldn't take his eyes from the vision of her lips caressing his manhood while her tongue drove him wild. Her gaze caught his and he saw triumph, desire, and mischief in her blue eyes.

He was seconds from coming, so he pulled her to her feet and swiveled her around so fast her hands automatically braced against the tile wall. Before she could even draw a breath, he slid into her from behind.

She shrieked and he froze, his skin chilling despite the hot water that flowed over him. "*Mierda.* Anna, I'm sorry. Did I hurt you?"

"No! Don't stop! That feels so amazing." She reached around and grabbed his ass to prevent him from pulling back. She even wriggled her hips to take him deeper.

He groaned. "Prepare for spectacular." He adjusted his angle, making sure to hit her G-spot with each thrust. One hand he slid down her front to toy with her clit while the other reached up and tugged on her nipples. She climaxed again, screaming his nickname. As her inner muscles clenched around him, they wrenched his own orgasm from the depths of his soul.

Anna Marquez owned him. Lock, stock, and two hard-as-rocks balls.

Chapter Twelve

Eduardo reached across and snagged his phone without waking Anna, who was draped across him like an abandoned blanket. He'd heard various footsteps outside his door for the past hour, but so far no one had knocked or attempted to enter.

He sent a text to Tiago who was undoubtedly already in Chile: *In bed. With Anna. Never leaving. Please ask your housekeeper to send food to my room.*

A second later he got a thumbs-up emoji.

Anna stirred as he replaced the phone. "Morning," she mumbled against his chest. "At least I assume it's still morning."

"Yup. How are you feeling?"

She pushed herself into a sitting position and gazed down into his face. A soft smile curved her lips. "No regrets."

"You're not too sore?" After the frenzy in the shower, he'd brought her to orgasm two more times in their bed but hadn't entered her again.

It was the best night of his life.

"Nope."

She settled back against him. "What time is it?"

"Ten thirty."

"Everyone must be wondering where we are." But

she made no attempt to move, instead snuggling against him, rubbing her cheek against his chest.

"I told Tiago we would spend the day in bed."

"That was very presumptuous of you," she said.

"Are you complaining?"

"No. Just reminding you that I don't like decisions being made for me. Speaking of which," she said, sliding off his chest and lying back against the pillows, "what are we going to do about our adversary? I say, let's draw them out and end this once and for all."

"And how do you suggest we do that?"

"I give a free concert at the local stadium."

"No way." She couldn't be serious. It would be suicide. "There's no way we could keep you safe with a crowd of that size."

"Then let me go back to LA. I'll hire extra security. If nothing happens, we know I'm not the target."

"And if it's your mother or one of Simon's children who is behind this, you'll be walking straight into the lion's den."

"At least you'll be safe." The love in her eyes dampened his anger a little.

"I can look after myself."

"Said many a dead man. How come you can look after yourself, but I'm too stupid to do the same?" She shifted to get out of the bed. He put a hand on her wrist.

"You're not stupid. Far from it. But you are famous. That comes with greater challenges." He ran his fingers up her arm to circle her elbow. "Anna, I know you're new to morning-after protocol, but this is not the way to start a day in your lover's bed."

That, at least, elicited a small smile. "I've always been one to buck the trend. However, for the sake of a well-rounded sexual education, how's it usually done?"

He tugged gently on her wrist, and she moved back to his side. "Whispered words of amazement at how awesome the night was. Example: 'You were fantastic, Eduardo, the best I've ever had.'" He trailed kisses up her arm to her collarbone. "A spoken reluctance to ever move or leave the bed, no matter what your bladder may be shrieking. Such as, 'I never want to move from your side. I will stay here forever.'" His lips slid down and hovered above her nipple, which had tightened already. "Then gentle caresses that awaken the senses"—he flicked her nipple with his tongue but didn't touch her elsewhere—"until one partner finally gives in to their body's demands and … runs to the bathroom."

Throwing back the covers, he darted to the adjoining room to her startled laugh. He turned on the bathwater as he passed.

By the time he emerged, Anna was up to her ears in scented bubbles in the tub.

He sat on the edge of the roll-top bath to enjoy the view. "This evening when they're back, we'll sit down with Jacques and Tiago and call the investigators in America and my police contact in Buenos Aires. Together we'll formulate a plan to get us both back to our lives safely. Agreed?"

"Agreed." She lifted a bubble-laden toe from the bath and ran it up the outside of his thigh. "That leaves us the rest of the day. Whatever shall we do?"

He dropped a kiss on her instep then stood. "I feed

you first. You're too skinny. Don't they have food in LA?"

After slipping on a pair of boxer shorts, he opened the bedroom door a crack. A feast awaited on a rolling cart outside the door.

"I eat. I also exercise a lot. It takes stamina to put on a two-hour concert five nights a week for eighteen months."

"It also takes stamina to spend the day in bed with me," he said. He popped a piece of *medialuna* into her mouth.

She finished the mouthful, but before he could add another she asked, "What are the protocols for asking difficult questions the morning after?"

"Don't do it. Do you want *mate* or coffee?"

He stood and so did she. Bubbles and water sluiced from her body in an erotic waterfall. "Coffee. But after we decide a way forward regarding our security situation, we talk about us."

Reluctantly, he agreed. Because the sooner he heard the words 'you're right, this is all we could ever be' from her lips, the sooner her could begin healing again and move on.

Until then, however…

***

Anna ran a brush through her hair for the tenth time, finally convinced she'd gotten all the tangles out. She stared at herself in the mirror. Aside from a rosy glow to her skin, which she could put down to a vigorous rubbing after a third shower that day, she didn't look much different.

She felt different, though. She felt amazing. Like she had everything she'd always wanted at her fingertips. All she had to do was reach out and grab it.

The morning bath had been followed by a naked feast. That had resulted in another shower. Tiago's water bill would be through the roof this month.

A nap had followed, but she'd awoken to Eduardo's lips making a leisurely tour of her torso, then her lower half.

Thank goodness the children were outside in the pool, making their own noises. Because with the way she had screamed Eduardo's name as he'd initiated her into the intimate act of cunnilingus, she might have frightened them. Eduardo hadn't been satisfied, however, till he'd made her scream his name one more time as he took her over the side of the bed.

Muscles she'd never known existed in her body ached. Each movement brought her back to the pleasure she'd experienced in his arms. No wonder both Maya and Vivi has secret smiles that crossed their faces from time to time.

Loving was done for the day, however. It was time to join the others. Raul had started an *asado* earlier in the backyard. The smells wafting up from the Argentinian barbecue were enough to lure even Eduardo from their love nest.

She pulled her hair into a high ponytail and added just a dash of makeup and a bit of lip moisturizer before pulling on the bright patterned maxi dress.

As she was about to leave the room, her cell phone rang. She found it under a scarf on the dresser but hesitated to pick it up, Eduardo's warning ringing in her ears. But according to the caller display, it was Janet, her personal assistant.

"Hello?" she answered, deepening her voice to disguise it.

"Angel, are you okay?" Janet's slightly panicked voice sounded as though it were coming from next door.

"I'm fine. Just being cautious. What's up?"

"I could ask the same of you. When do you expect to return? I'm fielding calls from everyone. But the real reason I'm phoning is because Devin had a slot open up in his schedule and is interested in producing your next album."

Whoa. Talk about hitting the jackpot. Devin was a rising star in the music industry. The last two albums he'd produced had gone diamond in the United States. He was a genius when it came to turning a good song into one that touched the heart and left a lasting impression. She got the tingles imagining what he could do with 'Hurricane Heart.' That he could resurrect her career in the process was an added bonus.

"When's his availability?"

"In five weeks."

"Five weeks? I've only got six new songs written."

"You had only two last time I asked. The fact that you've written four more in two weeks shows that you've got your spirit back. It's what Simon would want, you know—for your light to shine upon the world once more."

"I'm not sure…"

"Of course you are. I've told Devin you'd be delighted."

Anna had hired Janet because she wasn't overawed by Angel's fame and treated her as a human being. But sometimes, the lack of deference was a bit of a shock. Who worked for whom?

But before Anna could protest, Janet continued, "And I've promised that you'll appear at the Starlight Gala to benefit the children's cancer charity. You won't have to sing, just show up and look stunning. That's in six weeks. Let me know if you want me to find you a date, but given Simon's recent passing, going solo is fine too. The rest of your schedule I've left free for now, but I've got invitations stacked up almost as tall as me."

"Decline them all. I'm not in the mood to socialize. And if I'm going to be in studio soon, I've got my work cut out for me." Devin might be a genius, but he was also a taskmaster, demanding total commitment from his artists. She'd have to ramp up her vocal exercises and her cardio program. It was one thing to sing for a couple of hours a night. Once she began recording, she'd be expected to put in eight-hour days, and more if she was as distracted as she'd been lately.

Two men's voices came to her through the closed bedroom door. She couldn't hear what they said, but Eduardo's answering laugh was unmistakable. Dios, he'd been so wonderful the past couple of days, like the Eduardo she'd known before but with the added sexiness of experience.

"… a problem." Janet's serious tone brought Anna

back from her fantasies of Eduardo in the shower.

"What problem?"

"We made a major screw-up. We forgot to check the local weather when we were releasing photos of you in Europe. The last one we issued was taken in Budapest on a glorious sunny day. Problem is, it's rained nonstop in Hungary for the past three weeks. So the media knows you're not there. Now rumors are flying that you're in rehab. Or my personal favorite: you've been abducted by aliens, and we're covering until you're returned."

The alien thing wasn't far wrong. Except she hadn't been kidnapped: she'd willingly surrendered and submitted to the experimentation. And liked herself better for it.

"Say nothing for now. When I'm back next week, I'll explain that I returned to my homeland to bury my grandmother and took a few weeks to reconnect with my muse."

"Do you have a return date and flight times yet?"

"No. And don't tell anyone where I am. But you can stop issuing photos of me in Europe. Anything else?"

"Oh, yeah, your record label sent over an intern. She's the niece of some bigwig on the marketing side. Her name is Marsha Smith and she's really friendly and helpful. I'm sure you'll love her. At the moment, she's mostly just answering the phone and logging appearance requests. I thought I should let you know in case you called and didn't recognize the voice."

Mierda. Paranoia sent tingles racing through Anna.

"We'll talk about that when I get back. *Hasta luego*, Janet."

The knock on her bedroom door came as she put down her phone. Eduardo didn't even wait for her call to enter.

"Who was that?" he demanded.

"Not that it's any of your business, but I was talking to my personal assistant."

"I told you not to contact anyone."

Well, that was a quick transition from lover to custodian. "I didn't. Janet called me. Shall we go down to the others, or do you need a few minutes to get that pole out of your ass?"

He caught her wrist as she walked past him. "I'm trying to keep you safe. If something happened to you—"

"Look, I trust Janet with my life. But if I stay here, I have no life. I can't turn my back on everything just because some lunatic wants to scare me. Or is it you? We still haven't positively identified which of us is the target."

"The easiest solution to that is for me to go back to BA with Tiago tomorrow while you stay here in safety. If nothing happens, we'll know it's you they want. And we can then come up with a plan to resolve this once and for all."

"Meanwhile I just sit here and look pretty? That's not how it works these days."

He ran an agitated hand through his hair. "That's not what I meant and you know it. You're just trying to pick a fight so that when you walk away from me again, you can do it with a clean conscience."

Was he right? Was she subconsciously sabotaging

what they'd shared so she could go back to her old life without a backward glance?

Now wasn't the time to sort it out.

"They're waiting for us downstairs."

She tugged on the arm still held in his grasp. But instead of letting her go, he laced his fingers with hers. "I'm sorry. I shouldn't have lashed out at you."

"And I shouldn't have jumped on the defensive." She smiled up at him. "Look at us, being adults, resolving our differences right away." Except they weren't really resolved, only postponed.

"As we're both over eighteen now, we can make up properly," he said, lowering his head. His lips brushed hers, lightly at first then with more insistence. He released her just as she was forgetting how to breathe. "But since we've already ignored everyone for most of the day, we should show our faces now."

It took a moment before she could respond. "You're right. But remember where we left off. And you also promised that after we discuss our security situation, we can talk about us."

He nodded, but a hint of sadness flitted through his eyes.

Everything was in limbo. But when the situation was resolved, would she be reaching for heaven or staring down hell?

***

Eduardo scanned the crowd, searching for Anna. The children had dragged her away from him as soon as they'd set foot on the grass. Miranda had a new idea for a song and needed Angel's input.

He might as well get used to it. In the off chance they could somehow continue their relationship, there would always be people demanding her time and attention. And they wouldn't all be as cute as an eight-year-old, tiara-wearing, princess-dressed leader of two small boys.

Tiago had invited a few of the commandos who'd been guarding the place to the barbecue. One happened to be Vivi's father, who had recently transitioned to civilian life after years in the French elite army corps. It was easy to spot the military men among the fifteen or so gathered for the asado. Despite being dressed casually, they were still alert to any potential danger.

Which should mean that Anna was completely safe. Only a lunatic would venture this far onto a private estate surrounded by armed forces.

"Partnership meeting Friday at ten o'clock," Tiago said beside him. He'd been searching for Anna so intently he hadn't noticed his friend approach.

"That sounds ominous." He spotted the children, who were now pestering Jacques for rides on his shoulders. But still no sign of Anna.

"I need to know if I should keep my eye out for another partner. Vivi thinks Mendoza will be a better environment for Miranda's schooling, so we'll be spending the bulk of our time here soon. If you're going to be in LA or somewhere else in the world…"

"I'll be in Argentina." He saw a blonde head next to a tall, older man, but it was Vivi talking with her father.

"Will you? I won't think less of you if you follow your heart. I'd do the same in your position."

"Anna doesn't need me. She has people."

"Not one who loves her like you, who wants what's best for her, even if it doesn't make any money."

The itch up his spine grew more insistent. "Have you seen her recently?"

Tiago searched the group as well. "She was with the children a few minutes ago. They were singing a song Miranda wrote about a cat that drove a car." He signaled to Vivi's father, who was beside them in an instant.

"We can't see Anna."

With one hand gesture, all the commandos converged on their location. Vivi's father, Pierre, gave rapid instructions in French before they began to fan out around the grounds. Dusk was settling in, and shadows loomed large and eerie around the area where the barbecue had been set up.

Jacques, who was passing nearby with Max on his shoulders, stopped. He and Tiago exchanged a couple of words, again in French.

"Jacques is going to take the women and children inside," Tiago explained. "You and I will check the house. Maybe Anna's just gone back up to her bedroom to get a wrap or her guitar."

If she had, she was going to be pissed that he'd basically mobilized an army to find her. On the other hand, it would prove how seriously he took her safety.

The niggle up his spine had now turned into a raging torrent. Eduardo took the steps two at a time. Anna wasn't in her room, although her guitar still held pride of place on the chair next to her bed. She wasn't in his room either. Hope began to slowly bleed out of his heart.

The next thirty minutes were the longest of his life. He and Tiago searched the rest of the house in tandem. Jacques had taken up a defensive position on the stairs to the upper floor, where Tiago's home office and a hidden panic room were located. Vivi's father found them on the back terrace.

"One of my men has failed to check in. There are indications of a scuffle at his position. But no body or blood."

"And that's a good sign?" Eduardo could barely get the words out.

"Yes. It means whoever is doing this isn't after a body count. They want Anna alive."

How long that would last was the question no one wanted to answer.

Chapter Thirteen

Anna shifted, and a shaft of pain shot from her head down her shoulder, numbing her left arm. The noises she could hear were muffled. Everything was black. She tried to scream, but all that escaped was a hoarse *mmph* as the gag bit into the side of her mouth. Fabric pulled tight across her nostrils as she attempted to drag in a lungful of panicked air.

Her brain scrambled to come up with the who, what, where, when, why, and how of her situation. *Start with what you know, girl.* She'd been at the asado in Tiago's backyard. The children—*Madre de Dios*, the children. Were they okay?

A loud bang sounded beneath her, and a microsecond later her head connected with something hard. Her senses were sharpening, but everything was still fuzzy around the edges. *Have I been drugged?* The urge to slip back into oblivion was strong.

Focus on the facts. It felt like she was lying in the back of a moving vehicle, not one particularly well made. She struggled to sit up and knocked into a solid object. Another body? It was too large to be a child. Although at this point, she wasn't sure if that was good news or bad. She'd figured out the where, sort of. Now to figure out the how.

Back at the barbecue, the children had sung her a song and asked if she'd sing it with them after they'd all eaten. She'd promised, and then they'd raced off together to tell the other adults.

She'd lingered next to the rotunda in the rose garden where the children had put on their audition. She'd wanted to absorb all the feelings: the familiarity of an Argentine national past-time, the love and friendship of being with people who knew her as Anna and expected nothing more than kindness from her. And Eduardo, always Eduardo. He was so handsome in his jeans and light blue polo shirt that she wanted to stride over to him and claim him for the world to see. He'd consumed her senses, overthrown her world, awakened her to new possibilities. A song had popped, fully formed, into her brain.

She'd taken one step towards him…

Then woken up here.

The lump next to her moved again. "Are you okay?" it whispered. A man. Speaking French-accented English.

"Mm hm." She tried to mumble an affirmative.

"You are gagged, and there is something over your head. We are both tied up. We are in the back of a van, headed, it seems, up a gravel mountain road."

She tried to ask who he was, but all that came out was "ooh ahh ou?" Was he one of her captors, trying to make her feel better? But why?

"I am one of the commandos who didn't do his job very well. They got me first: a needle in the neck while I was distracted. I am not gagged and bagged like you. But I am tied up like a badly wrapped Christmas present." He sounded almost insulted that he hadn't merited harsher treatment. "These guys must be amateurs. Professionals would have blindfolded and muted the trained soldier, not the singing superstar. I'm a big fan, by the way."

Well, at least she wasn't alone. That would be more terrifying. Had Eduardo noticed her missing yet? Was he frantic? Angry that she'd wandered off when she knew her life was in danger?

Would she ever see him again? Hold him? Love him?

Her heart pounded in her chest. Panicking wasn't going to help, but it seemed all she could manage.

The vehicle took a sharp turn and she slid against the side of the van, which winded her.

"If you can, swivel your body so our backs are against each other. Then if we brace our feet against the sides, we won't slide around so much."

Must be nice to be so calm after being drugged and kidnapped. But she did as he suggested.

"Don't worry. Help is on the way," he said reassuringly.

She wanted to believe him, but since she still had no idea who was behind all this, it was hard to work out how they could be saved. Were they going to ransom her? Her money was mostly tied up in trusts and long-term investments. It would take weeks for her team to liquidate enough assets to pay a decent amount. Would her kidnappers agree to a payment plan?

A hysterical giggle welled up inside her. Imagine the press report if she were released for $250,000, three supercars, and six pairs of Manolo Blahniks, with an IOU for the rest.

"My name is Paul, by the way. May I call you Anna?"

"Mm hm," she replied.

He continued to talk softly, telling her that he'd been in much worse situations and they'd all turned out okay. She knew he was trying to reassure her, but from her point of view, it seemed like she'd been kidnapped with someone who routinely got himself in trouble. For a second, she wondered which of them had been the true target.

But she was no closer to figuring out who wanted her taken. Simon's children must know that even if she were out of the picture, their father had named two alternates to head up his foundation. The bulk of the money would never come to them. And despite what Eduardo had suggested, her mother couldn't be involved. Sure, they'd never really seen eye to eye, and the normal familial bond had been reduced to a monthly stipend.

Dios. Could her mother really want her dead? She was a beneficiary of Anna's will. Was this just a way to a bigger payout? *Why didn't she just ask me for the money? Would I have given it to her?* It was so screwed up. And now Paul was caught up in the middle of things. Although, in truth, he seemed happier about the current situation than she was.

"And then this one time I was in… Well, I guess I shouldn't tell you where I was. Let's just say the country name ended in *-stan*—"

The van came to a screeching halt, the back end sliding from side to side. She braced for impact and sent up a quick prayer that they didn't go over the edge of a mountain cliff. The loud *whump-whump* of a helicopter sounded nearby, and the vehicle rocked slightly from side to side with the downforce.

"See, I told you help was on the way," Paul said, way too calmly for the situation. "Lie flat. I'll cover you if there's gunfire."

She complied. Her breathing was erratic, and her heartbeat was too loud in her ears to hear anything. Was there shooting? Oddly, the silence was worse. At least in movies you had scary music to warn you.

The quiet went on too long. Even Paul, who lay almost on top of her, seemed tense.

Suddenly, the rear doors of the van were flung open. The blackness became slightly less oppressive. Was she being rescued? Or transferred to another vehicle?

Paul shifted off her. "*Salut, Capitaine.* I kept the subject safe, as promised."

"You were to prevent her from being taken, not go along for the ride." She recognized the voice of Pierre, Vivi's father. He'd come up to the house soon after Vivi had returned from France. "But good job activating your tracker device. We were able to follow you with ease."

Gentle hands helped her into a sitting position and carefully removed the fabric bag from her head. A large body dressed all in black blocked the bright light now flooding the back of the van. Was it daytime already?

"Is she okay?" Eduardo's worried question came from somewhere behind the man.

"Looks fine to me," Vivi's father called out, although he never turned from examining her. "There's no other way to do this. Sorry, it's going to hurt," he said. He peeled away one edge of the tape covering her mouth, then pulled it off quickly.

She could probably cancel her facial waxing appointments for the next ten years.

"Let me in." It was Eduardo again.

"Hold." The command in Pierre's voice halted even her breathing. "I need to make sure she's not wired with an explosive."

A nervous giggle escaped her. "Please do. I prefer dramatic entrances over exits."

Her body began to shake as adrenaline eked out of her system. For a day that had started with such promise in Eduardo's arms, it certainly had ended on a bum note.

Pierre patted her down. "Feel anything odd?" he asked.

She shook her head. Speech was impossible.

"Then I think you're good to go." He helped her to her feet, and she awkwardly made her way to the back of the van. The brightness she'd assumed was sunshine was a huge spotlight on the back of the Jeep parked across the mountain path. There was a pink tinge in the eastern sky, however, so dawn wasn't far away.

Six men in full Kevlar, with assault weapons at the ready, stood guard. Two other men dressed in black, their hands and ankles bound, sat on the ground with guns pointed at them. Her kidnappers, she assumed. But she didn't recognize them. At least it wasn't her mother and stepfather.

Before she'd crossed the bumper, Eduardo had her in his arms, striding towards the helicopter blocking the road ahead. His grip was hard on her thighs, the muscles against her body tense.

She opened her mouth, but the fierce look on his face froze the words on her tongue. If he blamed her for this, she was going to beg a ride back to Mendoza with Pierre.

The helicopter rotors were whirling again before the door was even closed behind them, and they lifted off the second her seat belt was latched. A set of headphones was placed over her ears and a bottle of water put in her hands. She turned towards her benefactor. "Wow, I didn't expect you to be here."

Vivi had a huge smile on her face. "I insisted on coming," she said. "I figured you'd want to see a friendly face, since all Eduardo has done the past twelve hours is scowl and bark at everyone." She leaned forward to check out the man who sat rigidly on Anna's other side. He did indeed still have a scowl on his face, his fists clenched either side of his thighs. Vivi's light laugh only tightened his lips. "Tiago is back at the villa having his own personal meltdown. I had to promise to stay in the helicopter or he threatened to lock me in my room until I'm sixty. Maya wanted to come as well. Jacques almost passed out when she suggested it. But she figured that her baby belly would get in the way of a good takedown."

Anna smiled, imagining the scene. "Weren't you afraid of triggering your PTSD?" Vivi had risked so much to come to her rescue.

"I've discovered that if children aren't involved, I'm fine." She inclined her head towards Eduardo. "I can't say the same about him. It was my job to secure him if things went sideways when we found you." There was a look in her eye that said the woman had skills beyond a few self-defense classes. And considering her father had been an elite army commando, she probably could keep Eduardo from doing something stupid. *Gracias a Dios*, it hadn't come to that.

He still sat like a statue beside her, his hands curled into fists. The only words he'd spoken were the six asking to see her in the van. He stared straight ahead, although the muscle pulsing in his jaw proved he still breathed.

"Any idea who took me?" Anna asked Vivi.

"Not yet. But my father will get the info out of the two back there. He's very good at that sort of thing. Even though he wasn't around much when I was a teen, I still never got anything past him."

Anna did not need details of how Pierre intended to extract the information. Her tremors became earthquakes, and Vivi pulled a blanket off the seat opposite and placed it around Anna's shoulders.

Eduardo snapped out of his trance at the movement and wrapped an arm around her, cradling her against his chest. The rhythmic beat of his heart beneath her ear, and whatever drugs were still circulating in her system, put her asleep before five minutes passed.

***

Eduardo struggled to pull in a deep breath. Tension still held him in its merciless grip. *Dios.* He'd come so close to losing her today. But what about tomorrow? Even if they'd finally caught the bastards who were targeting Anna, she still wouldn't stay. He'd heard her end of the telephone conversation with her assistant. Anna's life was back in LA. And it wouldn't wait much longer.

Meanwhile, he had three projects under construction, the community center demolition to get back on track, and a pitch to prepare for a new development in Montevideo. He'd be lucky to find five minutes to eat. There'd be no time to fly to LA for a booty call.

Anna stirred in his arms as the helicopter touched down in front of the mansion. As soon as the rotors slowed a little, the front door of the house flew open. Tiago raced to the chopper, wrenched open the door, and pulled his wife into his arms.

"I've decided. I am going to tie you to the bed," he said.

"Sounds like fun," Vivi replied with a laugh. She stopped whatever else Tiago was about to say with a lingering kiss on his lips.

Eduardo looked away. He'd seen his friend teeter on the edge of sanity when Vivi had been kidnapped. But at least he'd known that when he got his wife back, they'd be together. Anna may have been found safe, but there wasn't a happily-ever-after on their horizon. He ground his molars together to stop the shout that threatened to escape.

He sat Anna upright, slipped from the helicopter,

and lifted her into his arms to carry her into the house. She was so tiny, delicate. This could have had an entirely different ending.

"I can walk," she mumbled half-heartedly into his neck.

"Probably. But I don't seem to be able to let you go."

"Fair enough. Take me to your bed, Eduardo. I want to wake one more day in your arms." His heart thudded heavily in his chest. He wanted more than a day.

Jacques waited inside the foyer, his normally immaculate hair tousled. "Everything go okay?" he asked, concern in his voice.

Eduardo nodded, still not able to speak of the abduction without wanting to smash his fist through a wall. "As well as expected. Pierre is handling the cleanup."

"Perfect. I'm glad to see you're safe, Anna. The doctor is in the sitting room, ready to check you out. I'll go tell Maya. She wanted to wait here as well, but her ankles are swollen…" Jacques took the stairs two at a time.

"I don't need the doctor," Anna said as Eduardo headed towards the sitting room.

"Humor me, okay?"

The doctor was efficient in his examination. He drew a vial of blood so he could verify what she'd been drugged with. But as she was responsive and knew the date, her location, and Eduardo's middle name— Andres—the doctor figured she'd be fine following a good rest.

"Will you stay?" she asked after Eduardo laid her gently on his bed and began removing her shoes. His hands shook as he slid the dress from her body. Was this the last time he'd do that?

"I need to speak with Pierre when he returns." Even more important, he had to keep his focus on reality. Find who did this, crush them beyond recognition, and then let the woman he loved leave again.

Good times.

"Please." The plea he could never resist.

"I'll stay until you fall asleep. I have things to do."

"I'd like to be one of them." Her hands slid under his shirt as he lay next to her. Although her fingers were cold, they sent sparks racing across his skin.

"Anna—"

Whatever protest his brain was formulating died a sudden, swift death as her lips settled on his. She straddled him, her thighs spread wide as she lowered herself to rub against his growing erection. He'd left her underwear on in a vain attempt to either preserve her modesty or prevent himself having an aneurysm—his actual motivation was a vague thing. Now it just seemed stupid.

As if reading his thoughts, she reached behind her, unclipped her bra, and tossed it across the room. The hell of the past twelve hours was put aside as he glimpsed heaven.

He let her take the lead and set the pace, although it nearly killed him. She continued to grind her pelvis against his as she unbuttoned his shirt and kissed his chest as each inch of skin was revealed. He held onto her breasts, massaging them and plucking at her nipples, but she stayed too far away to allow him to feast on them with his mouth. By the time she had his shirt undone, he was panting beneath her.

His jeans were her next target. He tried desperately to recall rugby rules as she slid the zipper down with torturous slowness. For a woman who'd been a virgin thirty-six hours ago, she'd quickly learned how to drive him wild. He dutifully lifted his hips so she could shimmy off his pants and boxers. However, when he tried to flip her onto her back, she was having none of it.

Time ceased to exist as she explored his body with her hands and lips. There was something urgent he needed to do, but for the life of him, he couldn't remember what.

When eventually she slid down onto his rigid length, encasing him in her wet heat, he pulled her head down to his. "Dios, Anna. When I thought I'd never see you alive again…"

She put a finger over his lips. "I'm here. I'm safe."

He was going to have to learn to take what he could and be content with that. It went against his very nature. He'd always worked hard to get more. With Anna, that didn't seem to be an option.

She moved on him, and he relegated worries about tomorrow until then. Her gaze locked on his, their fingers entwined, and in a rare occurrence of synchronicity, they climaxed together. As they drifted back to earth, she flopped onto his chest and within a minute was fast asleep.

Eduardo joined Tiago in his home office twenty

minutes later.

"I didn't expect to see you until at least late afternoon," Tiago said.

"Anna's sleeping," he replied, knowing that would be enough of an explanation for his friend. "Has Pierre returned yet?"

"No, but he called. The thugs apprehended were hired by Theo Carsdale. That name mean anything to you?" As he asked, he poured Eduardo a mug of steaming coffee from a carafe on the sideboard.

Eduardo accepted the hot beverage with thanks. Having been awake all night worrying about Anna and then the 5:00 a.m. rescue mission, he was running on fumes of adrenaline.

"No. But according to Jacques's source, Anna's mother is involved in some shady business. It could be someone connected with that."

"Does that mean her mother is behind this?" Tiago refreshed his own coffee and sat back behind the desk.

"I hope not. Anna may not have the best relationship with her parent, but she's the only family she has."

"She has you."

He sipped the coffee, trying to get his brain and his heart to work in tandem. "I'm just a temporary stopover on her world tour. If her security issues are resolved, she'll be returning to LA by the end of the week."

"Is that what you want?"

"No, dammit. But you saw the way Vivi reacted when Anna sang. The world needs her songs."

"And you need her."

"Probably. But I've lived without her before. I'll do

so again."

Tiago opened his mouth then shut it again.

Change of subject required. "Did you have the Skype meeting with the woman from the community center protest group?" Eduardo asked.

"Yes, and it went very well. She's excited for the opportunities for the area's youth and has a lead on a suitable location. If we can get something to her in writing stating our commitment to sponsor the programs, she'll present it to the other members of her group. Providing all goes well, they'll endorse our planning application and we could be breaking ground as soon as next month."

"Excellent," Eduardo said.

That would coincide nicely with his upcoming personal breakdown.

Chapter Fourteen

Anna woke alone. The sheets next to her were cold. The curtains were drawn over the day. A couple of towels and a change of clothes lay waiting on the chair by the dresser. But there was no sign of the man who'd taken her heart. There'd be no rescue from that captivity.

Her holiday from regret was over.

Her head was still a little fuzzy, but the heaviness had gone from her muscles. A shower helped, although she spent most of the time under the water reliving her time there with Eduardo. Was this how it would be from now on—every little thing a reminder of him?

Not ready to face anyone just yet, she went to her bedroom. The myriad emotions clogging her brain function needed an outlet. She picked up her guitar and hit record on her phone in case she produced anything worth saving.

After an hour and a mishmash of melodies, she paused. Her legs were numb from sitting cross-legged, and she needed to stretch. A soft rap on the door halted her sun salutation.

"Yes?" she called out.

Vivi's head popped around the door. "Sorry to disturb, but we heard you singing, so I knew you were awake. Are you finished, or would you like more time alone?" Maya waved to Anna from behind Vivi.

She wasn't feeling up to the children's rambunctiousness just yet, but a few minutes with the two women who had so readily befriended her would be welcome.

"Come in." She gestured Maya towards the chair she'd just vacated. The woman waddled even more than she had the day before, and she was as barefoot as Vivi.

"The babies have shifted," Maya said. "Everything is fine, but we're going home this evening. I wanted to say goodbye before we left."

"I'm going to miss you all, but especially little Max."

Maya smiled. "He's one of a kind. Will you visit us in France? You're always welcome."

"When I'm next in Europe, I'll be sure to call." Anna attempted a smile; it appeared to work.

"You're going to keep touring, then?" Vivi asked, perched on the end of the bed. Now dressed in a bright yellow sundress, she seemed the antithesis of the black-clad, kickass ninja who had flown in on a helicopter to support Anna's rescue.

"What else can I do? I'm Angel."

Maya's eyes narrowed. "Angel should be part of who you are, not your whole existence."

A short laugh escaped. "You sound like Eduardo."

"I'll take that as a compliment. I know we've just met," Maya continued, "but I speak from experience when I say that it's never too late to reinvent yourself. If Angel isn't making you happy anymore, then become someone else. Anna seems pretty cool."

Anna's smile wavered. "I can't just walk away."

"No, I guess you can't. But remember to choose happiness. And sometimes that comes from saying no."

"Or saying yes to the right man," Vivi added.

Anna slumped onto the bed next to Vivi. "And if the right man hasn't asked the right question?"

Maya reached over and took Anna's hand in hers. "He won't ask you to give up your world for him. That decision has to come from you. Besides, the 'men have to ask' rule got overturned years ago. If you want him in your life, make the first move. Ask him where he'd feel comfortable."

"Oh, come on, Maya," Vivi said. "You ask any man *that* question and the answer is going to be 'balls deep inside you.'"

All three of them laughed. She was going to miss this girl time almost as much as she'd miss Eduardo. "He hasn't told me he loves me," Anna said.

"He does," Vivi replied. "You should have seen him yesterday when you disappeared. He was frantic."

"But I told him I loved him. He never said it back."

Maya gave her hand a squeeze. "Jacques didn't tell me he loved me until it became part of a revised relationship agreement."

Vivi's face twisted with a wry smile. "Tiago told me when he proposed that he would probably never love me."

"And you married him anyway?" Anna asked.

"It was a gamble, but it paid out magnificently," she said with a look only a well-loved woman could achieve.

As if by unspoken mutual consent, the topic of her

future and Eduardo's place in it was dropped. They chatted for a few more minutes about clothes and shoes, Maya lamenting the fact she couldn't get her feet into her favorite stilettos anymore.

Maya tried to get out of the chair, but it took both Vivi and Anna to help her stand. "I love being pregnant, but I think I'm ready to meet these two face-to-face." Her belly lurched visibly—no doubt the babies agreed. She rubbed her hands over the bump. "And yes, *mes enfants*, we will be having words about turning your mama's abdomen into your personal cage fighting ring."

"How much longer till you're due?" Anna asked. She'd always wanted children of her own, but it had seemed such a distant dream over the past years that she'd deliberately shut her mind to it.

"Six weeks officially. But at my appointment last week, the doctor said that both babies are a healthy weight. So if I go into labor early, there shouldn't be any complications."

Anna nodded. "Having watched Jacques fuss over you, I'm surprised he let you get on the plane at all."

Vivi rolled her eyes and chuckled, but it was Maya who answered. "He chartered a specialty plane with a surgical suite, hired an entire obstetrics team to fly with us, and purchased two state-of-the-art incubators," Maya said. "But his first wife died while pregnant, so I'm giving him a pass on his obsessive worrying this time."

Now Anna could better understand Jacques's preoccupation with Maya's health. "I hope everything goes smoothly," Anna replied. "You will let me know when they're born, won't you?"

Her friendship with these two women, although recent, was too precious to lose. She had a lot of people who worked for her, and many of them even cared. But it had been a long, long time since someone had accepted her without expecting anything in return. And even longer since she'd felt that being Anna was enough.

"Of course. And I meant what I said about visiting us in France. Jacques has very impressive security measures in place if that's still an issue."

"I'll keep it in mind." Anna opened the door and all three women filed out of the bedroom, halting when they saw Jacques, Tiago, and Eduardo waiting at the end of the hallway with another man.

"Daniel!" Maya waddled forward and flung herself at the newcomer. "Is Lexy with you?"

Ah, now she recognized Tiago and Jacques's brother, Daniel Michaud, the Formula 1 race-car driver and Max's soon-to-be stepdad.

"Of course," Daniel replied. He hugged his sister-in-law and wrapped an arm around her shoulders, tucking her against his side. "She's in the kitchen. Max is giving her a full recital of every car he's been in or seen since we left for the race in China."

Jacques peeled Maya off his brother and wrapped both arms around his wife from behind, his large hands resting protectively on her baby bump. A wave of longing swamped Anna, and she missed the first part of Tiago introducing her to Daniel.

"We've met," Daniel said. "She performed a concert after the Singapore Grand Prix a few years ago. Nice to see you again, Angel."

"I prefer to be called Anna by my friends," she said. She'd made the first steps to reclaim herself from her onstage persona; she wasn't going to stop now.

"Then Anna it is, if I'm to be honored as one of your friends," Daniel said, enveloping her in a friendly hug. From the corner of her eye, she saw Eduardo stiffen and take one step forward.

"Congratulations on your win in China. I didn't know much about Formula 1 before I performed at the concert. Now I'm hooked." Her gaze sought out Eduardo. "Although rugby will always be my number-one sporting passion."

Daniel, too, turned to look at Eduardo. "I can understand that. If you ever want to attend a race, just let me know and I'll get you a paddock pass."

"Thanks."

Eduardo moved next to her. "Anna, we need to talk about last night," he said quietly as the others engaged in a family reunion where people were actually happy to see each other.

She nodded, and they headed upstairs to Tiago's home office. Pierre Dubois, commando extraordinaire, stared out the glass door that led to a Juliet balcony. He was still dressed in his black fatigues, a steaming mug of coffee cradled in his hands. He turned as they entered the room.

"Thank you for rescuing me so promptly and efficiently," Anna said. What was the protocol here? Do you hug a mercenary? Send a bottle of scotch or a case of beer? Maybe a fancy gadget for an assault rifle?

"No problem. Although I apologize that you were

taken. I admit, I prefer action to waiting around for something to happen."

She could understand that. Although she'd had her fill of that particular brand of adventure for a few centuries. "Will it keep happening?"

"That rather depends on the outcome of this discussion," Pierre said. He nodded at Eduardo, who, with a hand at her waist, led her over to the sofa. He sat next to her, lacing his fingers with hers. She hadn't realized how cold she was until he touched her.

"What did you discover?" She was too squeamish to ask how they'd extracted the information.

"The kidnappers—who, by the way, were two of the most inept criminals I've come across—were hired by Theo Carsdale. Does that name mean anything to you?"

Anna shook her head. Odd. She'd always figured a person would know the name of their mortal enemy.

"He's a mid-level manager in an organized crime syndicate operating in the southwestern United States."

"Still not ringing any bells," she said. "Did one of my songs upset him?" Because aside from a couple of tour dates in the area a few years ago, she hadn't ventured into that part of the world since her late husband had become housebound.

"No, but your mother absconding with two-point-one million dollars of his money did."

"What?" She'd have leapt from the sofa if Eduardo hadn't kept a hold on her hand.

"It seems your mother was laundering money for him through the casinos. Only on the last run, she didn't return the clean cash. Evidently, Carsdale was hoping that after the incidents in BA, you'd get scared and run home to Mommy, thus revealing her location. They escalated to kidnapping, intending to leak your abduction to the media to lure her out of hiding or prompt an equivalent-sum payout by your management."

"Dios." She rubbed her temples with her free hand. This clearly wasn't the first time that Pierre had delivered shocking news, because he waited for her to sort through her thoughts and emotions before pressing for a response.

How dare her mother put her in this position? Was this all she could expect from her only living relative—to be a pawn in a game she didn't ask to join? The questions whirled inside her, plucking at her heart, tugging the air from her lungs as she tried to breathe.

"I haven't spoken to my mother in a long time," she said. After clearing her throat, she continued, "I fired her as my manager several years ago, and she wasn't happy. Although I put money in her account each month, our relationship has been very strained. She didn't call me when my husband died or come to the funeral…"

Eduardo released her hand only to slip his arm around her shoulders and pull her more tightly against him, lending her his strength. "Valentina Marquez has always been selfish," he said.

Out of instinct, she wanted to defend her mother. But the words wouldn't form. She'd come to the same conclusion years ago.

"How do you want to proceed?" Pierre asked. He now leaned against the desk. But even in a relaxed pose, there was a lethality about him that kept Anna's nerves on edge.

"What are our options?" Eduardo asked. *Our*. Some of the tension eased from her shoulders. She wasn't alone.

"Easiest way is to pay the missing money to Carsdale. He'll call off his thugs and no one needs to know anything."

Anna swallowed. "But my mother gets away with stealing, even though it's dirty money, and a criminal still gets to profit from other people's misery."

Pierre shrugged. "I said it was the easiest, not necessarily the most moral. I deal in tangibles: lives, property, assets. I leave the decisions about what is right and wrong to others."

"What else can we do?" she asked.

"I can locate your mother and make her hand over whatever remains of the laundered money to Carsdale. It will be up to him how he reclaims the rest. You may need to boost your security until the debt is paid in full. Unless he chooses to make an example of your mother for anyone else who attempts to swindle him."

That did not sound pleasant. She may not get on with her parent, but she didn't want her maimed or killed.

Pierre continued, "Or I find Valentina and turn in the money to the FBI. But I can't guarantee that your name will stay out of the press if we go the legal route." He hesitated a moment, and a blank mask replaced the friendliness in his expression. "Fourth option: I eliminate Carsdale, Valentina, or both." He said it with the detachment of someone who'd done similar, and more.

"We'd rather avoid any … eliminations," Eduardo replied.

Anna pulled in a deep breath. "So either I pay for my mother's crime, or my family drama becomes fodder for gossip columnists the world over."

"That's about it," Pierre confirmed.

"She stole two-point-one million?"

"Yes. But for repayment, expect to pony up more. These crime boss types are really keen on compounding interest. And not at a competitive interest rate. To be safe, you're looking at about two-point-five million if you can pay quickly."

"It will take me some time to get the cash together. Simon insisted I keep most of my money tied up in long-term investments. He said the music industry was too fickle to rely on a steady income for long."

"We'll get the money together by Friday," Eduardo said. "Can you contact Carsdale and make the arrangements to transfer it? I'm assuming it's an all-cash deal?"

"Yes, on both accounts," Pierre said. "Also, Carsdale had an inside woman on your team, Anna. Some intern using the name Marsha Smith. That's how they found your exact location. They traced a call between you and your assistant. I'd be surprised if she's still in your employ, but if she is, get rid of her. Do you want me to handle anything on that score?"

Anna shook her head while avoiding Eduardo's eyes, sure there was a condemnatory I-warned-you-about-that glare waiting for her.

Pierre pushed away from the desk. "I'll be in touch."

Anna was mildly surprised that he used the door and not the window to exit the room.

***

Eduardo pulled Anna onto his lap while he still had the opportunity. A tremor shook her body, and her hands were like ice.

"I could get a loan with my next album as collateral," she said.

"That won't be necessary. I've got the money."

She raised her head and stared at him. "You've got two and a half million US dollars just lying around your apartment?"

"No. But I recently sold one of my investment properties in order to purchase another. I would rather spend that money keeping you safe."

"Eduardo…"

He put a finger over her lips. "Let me do this for you … for old times' sake."

"And new times?"

"Those too."

"Do they end here?"

He slid her from his lap and strode over to the window. If they didn't end this now, cleanly, they both risked living the rest of their lives in limbo.

"Yes. They have to. Your life is in LA or touring the world. Mine is here in Argentina."

"They're just places, Eduardo. After this album is

finished in about three months, I can move back here—
"

"Until it's time to tour. Then you'll be gone for up to a year, possibly two."

"You could come with me."

He shook his head. "No. I've worked too hard to get where I am now. I can't live my life orbiting your star. I have to be my own man."

"You were the one who told me two days ago that I couldn't stop singing. That people needed me."

"And that's still true. Anna, we knew going into this affair that it was just a temporary reunion. We both got what we wanted from it. You've solved your intimacy dilemma and experienced enough emotional highs and lows to write a new album. I got closure. Let's say a proper goodbye this time and go back to our lives with happy memories."

"You won't even try?" The pain in her voice sliced through his heart. No, *sliced* was too clinical, too clean-cut. It dragged him behind a tractor on a gravel path until he had road rash on his soul.

He ran a hand through his hair. "I have employees for whom I'm responsible. I have plans and dreams that won't be fulfilled following you around the world. I've worked since I was six years old. I'm finally making a name for myself. I can't… I won't give that all up to be known as Angel's boyfriend."

"What about Angel's husband?"

A brief flare of hope was extinguished by a memory of his father's face in his last days. "That either."

"I love you, Eduardo. I don't want to say goodbye."

Every instinct told him to take her in his arms, kiss her senseless, and whisper his devotion to her until their last ten years apart were a distant memory. *Dammit.* Why couldn't she just smile and walk away? Did he have to bare his entire soul? "You loved me before and left."

"But I didn't know then that it would be for so long. I always thought…" Her voice broke. He couldn't look at her. Her misery already echoed within him, growing, expanding until everything ached.

"This time you know. We'll always be special to each other. But we have to move on." Or at least she did. He wasn't sure he'd be able to.

She crossed the room to stand in front of him. "Why won't you tell me you love me?"

Direct hit.

"I told you before. It didn't make a difference."

"And if it does this time?"

He tugged on his hair until it hurt. "What difference can it make, Anna? We can't turn back time. Even if you gave up singing and touring, you'll still be Angel to the world. I'd be known as the man who destroyed a national treasure. What the hell do you think that would do to my reputation? Besides, I've watched you this past week. I've seen the seeds of a song take root in your heart. I've seen you carefully nurture them until pure magic slips from between your lips. That's not going to go away if we say 'I do' to each other. Music will always be inside you, looking for an escape. One day, another golden opportunity will come along. And it will either lure you away from me again…" He paused to pull in a painful breath. "Or you'll stay and hate the restrictions our love has put on who you really are. You'll crumble before my eyes, and I won't be able to bear it, knowing I've broken you."

Tears streamed down her face unchecked. "So this is it?"

"It has to be."

"You're breaking my heart."

"I'm sorry."

He walked away before he fell apart.

Chapter Fifteen

Tiago snapped shut his laptop, bringing Eduardo's attention back to him. They'd spent the last two hours in the Buenos Aires head office of Alva-Suarez Developments, performing a detailed analysis of all current and potential future projects, setting deadlines and allocating responsibilities.

As they'd finished, Tiago had taken a call from Vivi, and Eduardo had allowed his mind to wander. What was Anna doing now? Was she happy back in LA?

"You've become a self-fulfilling prophecy," Tiago said.

That did not sound like a compliment. "What the hell does that mean?"

"You expect every woman to leave you. So you don't give them a reason to stay."

"If you're referring to Anna, she was always going to leave." Eduardo closed his own laptop, ready to depart before this conversation ended with two men in suits brawling on the floor of a glass-walled boardroom.

Tiago speared him with a look Eduardo had seen him use on Miranda when she was getting cheeky. "She'd leave Argentina but not you."

"What's the difference? My life is here." He rubbed a hand across his clavicle. It ached like the devil. Which was odd, as the day was nothing but sunshine.

"You can be a man anywhere in the world, you know. Life is mobile."

Maybe too much marital bliss was softening Tiago's brain. "I feel it's my duty as your friend, business partner, and former solicitor to remind you that the reason I am in my current position is so you can spend more time with your family. There is also something in there about moving back to Mendoza to allow for Miranda's schooling and to expand the winery. Have you changed your plans?"

"No. However, a partner who stares moodily out the window during meetings isn't helping me do any of those things."

"You were on the phone with your wife!" Damn, he'd just admitted to staring moodily out the window. Good thing Tiago wasn't a lawyer and probably wouldn't catch that confession.

"Ha! You concede that you were lost in morose thoughts." Eduardo had trained him too well. Before he could open his mouth to refute it, Tiago continued, "And I don't need to be a mind reader to know you were thinking about Anna. My phone call lasted thirty seconds. You were staring out the window for five minutes."

"What if I was thinking about her? I'm still doing my job. Did you not read my thirty-page report on the Montevideo opportunity?"

"I did. I also noted that you saved that report to the server at four in the morning. You're not sleeping, barely eating from the look of you, and I haven't seen you smile since we left Mendoza."

"I—" Eduardo's assertion that he'd get his life together soon halted when Tiago raised his hand. He'd gotten over her leaving before. He'd do it again. Of course, the last time he'd been in the hospital with a handy button that injected him with morphine whenever the pain was too much. As a precaution, he'd asked his housekeeper to remove all alcohol from his apartment and had placed a photo of his father on his desk to remind him of what would happen if he wasn't careful.

"Listen," Tiago said, waiting until he had Eduardo's attention again before continuing. "I'd rather have a happy friend than a miserable business partner, even one as brilliant as you. We can make other arrangements. And there are ways you can remain a partner at Alva-Suarez. We're two smart guys, Eduardo. I'm sure we can come up with a solution so everyone can be happy."

Eduardo nodded. He took risks in business and succeeded. Wasn't it time to take one in his personal life? Because things for damn sure weren't working the way they were.

He needed to put the past firmly behind him and make his future the one he wanted.

It was time to make a new plan. One that included Anna.

***

Something about wearing a hard hat and handmade Italian leather shoes made Eduardo feel like a real man. Maybe it was the implied combination of hard work and success that spoke to him. Today, however, he felt like a fraud.

A real man didn't hurt the woman he loved. A real man fought for her, put her needs before his own, sacrificed whatever was required. A real man would never have let Anna go.

All his stupid talk about his dreams not being fulfilled if he followed her around the world. Not being able to live while hanging onto her... What a load of crap. He was nothing without Anna. He could rule the world, and it would be meaningless if she wasn't in his life. It was time he did something about that.

The old community center was surrounded by tall, blue, metal fencing with warning signs posted every five meters. It was a token attempt to keep people out. But at this hour of the day, with dawn just breaking over the horizon, he was the only one around except for the elderly security guard who dozed on a plastic chair that had one leg shorter than the others.

Eduardo had been scouting the area for half an hour now, trying to find a way in that didn't require scaling the fence in his suit. Next time he engaged in a break-and-enter, he'd dress more sensibly.

His hands tightened on the hammer he carried. In four hours, the area would be swarming with people and heavy equipment ready to demolish the building where he'd met Anna. Where they'd fallen in love.

For years, he'd wanted to destroy the reminder of what had been. Only now did he know the memories were etched too deeply into his psyche to be erased by the destruction of concrete and metal. He would love

Anna until the day he died, building or no building.

So what would a real man do?

He'd go after his woman.

Eduardo whirled around at a noise behind him, automatically raising his hammer.

"Are you going to take the center down by hand?" Tiago's amused voice was at odds with his hands-up defensive gesture. "If so, you're going to need something bigger than that little thing."

"You should know better than to sneak up on a man holding a weapon." Eduardo lowered the hammer, although his fingers were still clenched tightly on the handle. His gaze roamed over his friend. Why was Tiago here? Instead of being dressed in his usual suit, Tiago wore jeans, work boots, and a T-shirt under a leather jacket. "I haven't seen you up this early since your marriage."

"And I would still be wrapped around my soft, warm wife if I hadn't received a phone call half an hour ago that some weirdo was roaming the grounds of a building about to be demolished."

"I object to the term weirdo."

"You're wearing Armani to a demolition site. Every normal person knows Gucci is the dress code for destruction. Nice touch with the hard hat, though."

Eduardo cracked a fake smile. "Gucci for demolition, Armani for erection, got it."

Tiago scaled the fence then undid one of the clips from the inside so Eduardo could squeeze through. He waved a hand at the security guard, who evidently hadn't been as asleep as Eduardo had assumed. It wasn't until they were closer that he noticed the gun in the older man's hand. They both showed their IDs to him and were allowed to pass.

"So, what are we after?" Tiago said as he pushed open the front door. "I thought everything of value had been cleared from the site."

"Just a personal memento," Eduardo replied.

"Want me to wait here?"

"If you don't mind. I'll only be a minute."

He slipped the chisel from his pocket and returned within five minutes to where Tiago waited.

"What are you going to do with that?" Tiago asked.

"Hopefully, convince Anna to give me another chance."

Tiago slapped him on the back. "About time."

Dios, he hoped he wasn't too late.

***

"That's a good one, Angel. We're done for today." Devin's brusque tone came through her headphones. She slipped them from her ears and hung them on the stand next to the microphone.

She'd been back in Los Angeles for six weeks now. She hadn't seen Eduardo since he'd walked out of Tiago's study. According to Raul, he'd headed straight to the airport and back to BA to deal with an urgent situation.

Within two days of their goodbye, Pierre had contacted her and said all was clear on his end. So she'd flown back to America with Daniel, Lexy, and Max, who had been promised a trip to Disneyland.

What Pierre had done to clear up her situation, she had no idea. Nor any desire to know. Her mother hadn't called. Eduardo hadn't called. She'd instructed her accountant to liquidate some of her investments and wire the money to Argentina. An acknowledgment had come through from Eduardo's office that the funds had been received. But there had been no personal note from her former lover. No query as to how she was getting on. Oh, well, at least she didn't have to lie and say she was fine.

The only person who had called since she'd left Mendoza was Maya. She'd had her babies, a boy and a girl they'd named Charlie and Yvette. They'd arrived three weeks earlier than expected but well past the time when Maya had wanted them evicted for bad behavior. Everyone was well, although Jacques was reported to still be in a daze.

How long it would take Anna to recover from her visit to Argentina was anyone's guess. She still dreamed of Eduardo every night when she eventually fell into a restless sleep, and she woke alone and aching every morning. She couldn't cry; it would ruin her voice. She had an album to record. Or, rather, Angel did.

Anna had begun to resent her alternate persona.

She was back to dressing in white or pastels. Her hair was coiled in a neat chignon at her nape. Undoubtedly, a white Rolls Royce waited for her at the curb to whisk her to her secluded mansion among the clouds.

Not once growing up did she think she'd miss her

overcrowded, dilapidated apartment in Boca.

Enough. Poor rich girl, suck it up and get on with it. At least the album was going well. Devin loved her new songs. As she'd predicted, he'd arranged 'Hurricane Heart' in such a way that even the scary-looking sound mixer with innumerable piercings had been in tears when they'd played the final track.

Plastering her trademark smile on her face, she exited the recording booth to meet up with those who waited in the mixing studio.

"This album is incredible," her assistant Janet gushed. "Your best ever."

"Thanks." Anna was pleased with the work, but she still hadn't figured out how she was going to sing about Eduardo in front of thousands of people every night without going insane.

"Have you made a decision yet on a new manager?" Janet asked. As Pierre had predicted, the intern the record label had sent had mysteriously disappeared before Anna returned from Argentina.

"Not yet. You'll be the first to know when I've chosen." A lot of great people had contacted her, but no one Anna wanted to trust with her career.

Janet nodded. "How many more songs to record?"

"Three." One more lament, then the two happier songs Anna had written in those few days when she'd ridden high on the tide of Eduardo's attention. She'd left those for last. It was easier to sing about pain and suffering when that's what she felt.

"At this rate, we'll be done next week. I may even have time for a vacation." A rare smile crossed Devin's face.

"Excellent. So can I steal Angel away now?" Janet had already pulled out that tablet that Anna knew contained a very detailed schedule of all the things she was supposed to do. So far, she'd been able to plead exhaustion to escape all but the most 'vital' appearances.

"Yes," Devin replied. "The voice track is done. I want to play around a bit with some of the backing vocals. In fact, take tomorrow off as well, Angel. Rest your voice. We're tackling 'Penitent' next. Did you hear the revised arrangement I suggested? It's going to take your full range to knock it out of the park."

She had, and she was looking forward to the challenge. The song was even more personal now, because she had more to regret. The emotion should be easy to convey. Whether she could do it without crying would be the kicker. "I love the new sound. And I'll be ready. See you on Thursday."

Janet didn't even look up from her tablet. "Can you start in the afternoon on Thursday? Angel has the Starlight Gala tomorrow night and may be out late."

Damn. She'd forgotten about that. If it wasn't to benefit kids with cancer, there was no way she'd show.

"Sure. Let's say one o'clock," Devin answered. "If you need more time, give me a call."

Her life was being arranged around her. She really should protest, but that took too much energy.

Janet snagged Anna's handbag off the sofa and passed it to her, linked their arms, and nodded to the plain-clothes bodyguard Pierre had sent to watch out for Anna. It wasn't Paul, her fellow captive, with his cheery commentary. This guy's name was Claude or something, although in her mind Anna had taken to calling him Mr. Mute. She wasn't even sure he spoke English.

Janet tucked her tablet in her oversized handbag. "I've got a selection of ball gowns for you to choose from at the house. And it's not too late if you want to take a date. Dennis is back in town and available. He's always good for a laugh."

Dennis was the latest Hollywood heartthrob. They'd done a talk show together before he'd hit the big time with his last movie. So far, he hadn't gotten too egotistical, preferring to make people laugh instead of expecting them to bow to his talent.

He was fun. She just wasn't in the mood for company she'd have to be nice to. "I don't want to go with Dennis."

"Okay, then. How about—"

They were out on the street now, and Anna reached into her purse to find her sunglasses. She looked first at Janet, who had stopped talking and walking mid-sentence. Then she looked at the object of her assistant's stunned gaze.

"—him?" Janet finished her comment, although her mouth remained open.

Yes! Him! Anna's body screamed. She blinked. Twice. But it really was Eduardo who leaned against the back door of her waiting car. He was wearing a navy blue suit, baby blue dress shirt, and dark brown shoes. The buttons at his neck were undone, and a gray tie had been shoved into his pocket.

He straightened.

"Janet, I'll see you at the house. Tomorrow. No earlier than noon." Anna's voice was remarkably calm for a woman whose heart was pounding loudly enough to be picked up on Devin's recording equipment inside the building. Her eyes were too busy devouring Eduardo to see if her assistant was even still there. Because if Anna was hallucinating, she did not want to lose the vision.

She took two steps towards him, her gaze glued to his. Her heart, which couldn't take much more of a battering, made her ask, "Are you here with bad news? Or just to give me something I forgot?" His sexy smile weakened her knees, but she stood firm.

"I'm here to tell you something. I hope you won't think it's bad news. And I'm here to give you something. But it's something I forgot, not you."

"Now I'm confused."

He reached out and caressed her cheek, his thumb lingering for a moment on her bottom lip. A sigh came from somewhere next to her.

"I came to tell you that I love you. Irrevocably. Eternally. Absolutely."

"All approved adjectives. Definitely good news."

"And I want to give you this." He reached into his pocket and pulled out an item wrapped in an old-fashioned handkerchief. The oddly shaped object was heavier than she expected.

She unfolded the fabric. "You brought me a lump of concrete?"

"Turn it over."

A+E para siempre was written on the plaster on the

other side, within a badly drawn Sharpie heart.

"This is from the community center," she said through a thick throat. "You drew it on the wall after the first time we kissed."

"I knew then that I loved you and always would. I saved it from demolition. I didn't want to forget again. In this case, graffiti doesn't lie. Our love is forever, Anna. Whatever it takes to make it work. Wherever, whoever I have to be to make you happy. I'm in for the long run. *Para siempre*." Forever.

A tiny sob broke from Janet, who'd never left. "You guys are killing me," she said. "Get in the car before someone takes a photo and I have to spend the next twenty hours fielding calls about Angel's mystery man. I'll see you tomorrow afternoon at the house."

Bodyguard Claude got in the passenger's seat, and Eduardo held the door while Anna climbed in the back. Janet waved from the pavement, tears streaming down her face.

"Is she okay?" Eduardo asked.

"Janet is a romantic," Anna said as she pressed the button to raise the privacy screen between them and the front seat.

She should have asked what had changed since she'd last seen him. And she would, just as soon as she finished kissing him. Because, well, priorities were important.

His lips were on hers the second the seat belt clicked. Strapped into the back, it was an awkward embrace, but it felt like heaven.

"How long till we get to your place?" he asked as

he nibbled down her neck, his fingers pulling her top down her shoulder as he went. She wanted to rip the whole thing off, to feel his mouth on her skin, her breasts, everywhere. But the privacy screen wasn't private enough for that activity.

"About an hour, depending on traffic."

He sat back in the seat. "I guess that means we have time to talk."

Reluctantly, she readjusted her top and rested against the leather upholstery. Damn, he was good. She hadn't even noticed he'd undone her bra.

Kissing done. For now. It was time for sensible Anna to take control. "Did you mean what you said? You're here to try and make things work with us?"

"Tries only count in rugby. I'm here to succeed in loving you."

"How? I thought you couldn't be a man who trails around after me. Do you want me to quit singing?"

"No. I have a plan to present to you. Except my laptop is at the hotel I checked into."

"Can't you just tell me?"

"I'm more persuasive with PowerPoint." He waggled his eyebrows, and she burst out laughing.

"You're most persuasive with your lips on my body. But, since I have a feeling I should be lucid for this discussion, perhaps talking is a better idea."

"All right. But I spent hours on the presentation. You have to let me show it to you later."

She nodded. His good mood was both infectious and scary. Could they make this work? How could they not? The past weeks had been hell. She didn't want to spend the rest of her life in that misery. "What's your plan?"

"Are you still without a manager?"

"Yes." She knew she had to replace Simon, but it was too much to contemplate at the moment. Janet was good at what she did, but this was a job beyond her skill set. A manager had control of her entire life, her career…

"I'd like to apply for the position."

Hired! But she had to pretend to think about it, or he'd know how desperate she was.

"But you already have a job." She deepened her voice to mimic his. "Businesses and employees rely on you."

"And now they rely on a guy named Pablo Montoya. He's a friend of Tiago's late father. He has decades of experience in commercial property development. He retired two years ago to be with his wife, who was ill. But she's passed, and he's anxious to keep busy. So he took my job, and now I'm kind of unemployed."

She did her best to hide her smile. "You don't know anything about the music industry."

"I can learn. And there is one thing that puts me ahead of any other candidates. I know you. And I know what makes you happy. That will be my overriding consideration when faced with decisions: will this make Anna happy? And I mean that. Anna—not Angel. It's time you left her on the stage and regained some of what makes *you* special."

Safety be damned. She had a man to kiss. She undid her seat belt and launched herself into his arms. "You've got the job. I want to keep singing, but I don't want it to be all that I do. Together, we can find a balance. And you know what makes Anna happiest of all?"

"Being in my arms?"

"*Siempre.*"

Epilogue

Eduardo waited in the wings as the last note faded into the night. Outdoor concerts were always the most difficult, logistically and acoustically. But there was something magical about the music soaring to the stars above as though returning home. And Angel concluding her sold-out, two-year tour in La Bombonera, Boca's famous stadium, had both sentimental and practical significance. They were back where they'd started. And they could fly to Mendoza tonight with ease.

Fans screamed Angel's name as she waved her way off the stage. She'd be exhausted, he knew, especially after six encores that took the concert into its third hour. But she'd also be so high on performance adrenaline that it would be hours yet before she could relax.

He didn't have that problem. All he needed to relax was to wrap his arms around her and send up another prayer of thanks that he'd made the right choice and followed his heart. The past thirty months had been the best of his life. He woke every morning with Anna next to him, worked alongside her each day, and watched as she transformed into Angel, singing superstar, delighting thousands with her songs.

"Amazing concert," he said into her ear. "As always. You sure you're ready to give all this up?"

"I'm sure," she replied. "I know a way to keep busy." Her lips captured his in a blistering kiss that promised so much more once they were alone.

'Hurricane Heart' had broken sales records within a month of release, only to be eclipsed by 'Penitent' when it debuted on the airwaves. Anna was taking a break from her career at its pinnacle. Her choice. She wanted a baby. Or two. Or three.

They had some catching up to do. Maya had recently delivered her second set of twins. Two boys this time. Everyone was doing fine, including Jacques, who was by now an expert at changing diapers. Tiago and Vivi had an almost-two-year-old boy for Miranda to dote on and had just announced another pregnancy. Even Daniel and Lexy had gotten in on the family expansion business and produced a girl a year ago, much to Max's delight.

Eduardo and Anna had been adopted into the ever-increasing de Launay-Michaud-Alvarez clan. Anna's mother had never bothered to contact the daughter who had, in essence, saved her life. He knew it had bothered Anna for the first few months. But with the constant reassurance of his love and the whirlwind that accompanied launching a new album, she'd been too happy and too busy to worry about a woman who'd never really wanted her in the first place. The money she used to send her mother now went to Vivi's educational charity for impoverished children in Central America. And they both had a more loving family than the ones they'd been born into.

Raul and Timo were also included in the extended family celebrations when they took place in Mendoza. A judge had granted Raul full custody before Eduardo had left to follow Anna to LA. Raul's ex-wife's ties to a criminal organization were considered too risky to allow her even supervised access to her son. The two had moved to Mendoza permanently, where Raul worked for Tiago in the winery and Timo went to school with Miranda.

Eduardo's own transition to Angel's manager had not been without its challenges, but he'd relished them. By the time her tour had kicked off, he'd learned most of the ins and outs of the music industry. And, with the assistance of seasoned professionals, they'd ridden the highs and clung together during the lows of a volatile entertainment sector.

He'd also taken the opportunity afforded by their travels to study the real estate market globally. He was now perfectly placed to direct Alva-Suarez Developments' international acquisitions department, a position he would take up a month from now. After a much-delayed honeymoon.

Their wedding, at Jacques and Maya's chateau in France nearly two years ago, had been a small, family-only affair. Anna believed that her abuela had been looking down from heaven with a huge smile on her face and an "I told you to hold tight" on her lips.

And hold tight they did. Anna melted against him, her stamina depleted from having danced and sung for hours. He held her against him as the roadies began to pack up the show. The crowd at last realized that Angel wasn't going to reappear and started to disperse. They always stood like this for at least ten minutes after the show, a ritual that allowed Angel to transform once more into Anna.

"I'm looking forward to being an executive wife for a change," she said, gazing up adoringly into his eyes. "It'll be my turn to stand at your side while you charm everyone to your way of thinking."

"You will always outshine me. Not only with your beauty but your kindness and strength."

"Then we'll make quite a team. Because I only have those things because of you. I love you, Eduardo. And always will. Even if Angel never takes the stage again, I'll have no regrets. Thank you for letting me live my dream. Now I want to help you fulfill all of yours."

It was his turn to capture her lips until they were both breathing heavy.

"You make my dreams come true every morning when I wake next to you." He nodded his head towards a few diehard fans who stood at the edge of the stage, still calling for Angel to reappear. "Are you sure you're not going to miss people screaming your name?" he asked as he lifted her in his arms to carry her to her dressing room.

A sexy smile curved her lips while she slid a hand down his back to cup his ass. "I'm only interested in one man calling my name. And it's not Angel I want to hear from his lips—it's Anna. If it's accompanied by declarations of love and devotion, all the better."

He tightened his arms around her.

"*Para siempre.*"

~~~~~~~~

Thank you for reading *The Developer and The Diva*. Please post a review where you purchased the book. Your opinion will not only help other readers decide whether to buy the book or not, it will also help me continue to write the stories that I, and hopefully you, love to read. Many promotional opportunities are only available after a book has a certain number of reviews. Please help me access these. Thank you!

Penitent

You'll never know what it cost me
To say these words to you
I'm sorry 'bout the way things ended
I should never have run from you

I'm penitent
My heart is full of regret
My conscience oh how it pains me
How can I ask you to forget?

I thought I'd paid the price
For pride and avarice
But then I saw you once again
And I remembered all the bliss

I regret the way things ended
I regret not being sure
This was a love to last forever
A love I should've held secure

I'm penitent
My heart is full of regret
My conscience oh how it pains me
How can I ask you to forget?

And now I have the chance
To atone for all my sins

But penitence is painful
And for your answer I'm on pins

I know that I'm not worthy
I know that it's not fair
That I'm asking for forgiveness
That I still want your life to share

I'm penitent
My heart is full of regret
My conscience oh how it pains me
How can I ask you to forget?

Have you read the other books in the Vintage Love series?

The Vintner and The Vixen (Vintage Love Book One)

It's all fun and games until someone falls in love.

Maya Tessier needs a fresh start after her last boyfriend dragged her deep into an organized crime ring, putting her life in danger. After inheriting a cottage and acreage in France from her great-grandmother, she hopes to escape her turbulent past to concentrate on her art. Unfortunately, her inheritance is within the estate of a privacy-obsessed billionaire. And he wants it all back.

Jacques de Launay has led a life of rigid control, working hard to repair the family's fortunes after his playboy father nearly destroyed them. His one attempt at happiness ended in tragedy when his pregnant wife was killed in a car crash. He'd rather be the last in the illustrious de Launay family line than open himself up to that kind of heartache again. Then Maya Tessier arrives on his doorstep and he discovers it's not only the ancestral land he wants to reclaim.

But if he lets her stay, more than his heart may be at risk.

Available now at all major online retailers. Visit https://alexia-adams.com to read an excerpt.

The Playboy and The Single Mum (Vintage Love Book Two)

He lives in the spotlight. She has to exist in the shadows.

If Formula 1 racing driver Daniel Michaud is to win the championship, he must steer clear of all distractions. However a compromising photo has his sponsor demanding that he be chaperoned for the rest of the race season. It's bad enough a sexy advertising executive is assigned to accompany him, but then they're joined by her adorable car-obsessed son. It's all Daniel can do to keep his mind on the track and off the tantalizing taste of love and family that could destroy his career.

Lexy Camparelli blames the Formula 1 circus for her parents' divorce and the obsessive eating disorder that ruined her teenage years. To keep her job, she's forced back into that high-stakes world. At least her heart isn't in jeopardy, given Daniel's playboy reputation. Then she discovers the gorgeous driver's secret and it's a race to see if Lexy can emerge victorious or lose everything—including custody of her son.

Available now at all major online retailers. Visit https://alexia-adams.com to read an excerpt.

The Tycoon and The Teacher (Vintage Love Book Three)

He'll do everything he can to avoid love. It may not be enough.

Argentinian tycoon, Santiago Alvarez recently lost his sister, brother-in-law, and father. Now he's solely responsible for his traumatized niece, Miranda, who hasn't spoken for three months. His only hope to help Miranda recover is a woman who tempts him like no other. Whatever it takes, he'll live up to his promise to care for his sister's daughter—even if it means marriage.

French teacher Genevieve Dubois is slowly recovering from post-traumatic stress disorder after the death of a student. Her new position, helping a little girl find joy again, brings with it an unusual complication—a super-sexy uncle who awakens Genevieve's desire for a family of her own. When her employer proposes marriage so he can keep custody of Miranda, Genevieve accepts, hoping to turn their passion into love. But when she discovers the real reason Santiago wants to be guardian of his niece, it threatens all their futures.

Available now at all major online retailers. Visit https://alexia-adams.com to read an excerpt.

Thank you, Reader

I hope you enjoyed reading Eduardo and Anna's story as much as I enjoyed writing it. If you did, **please, please** help others find it by leaving a **review** at your favorite retailer. Your review doesn't have to be long, but your opinion matters to me and other readers.

Want to be one of the first to know about upcoming releases, contests, and events? Sign up for my monthly newsletter at https://alexia-adams.com.

You can also chat with me on Facebook (https://www.facebook.com/AlexiaAdamsAuthor) and Twitter (@AlexiaAdamsAuth) or, of course, get in touch with me via my website (https://alexia-adams.com).

I love to hear from readers, so don't be shy.

About the Author

Alexia Adams was born in British Columbia, Canada and travelled throughout North America as a child. After high school, she spent three months in Panama before moving to Dunedin, New Zealand for a year where she studied French and Russian at Otago University.

Back in Canada, she worked building fire engines until she'd saved enough for a round-the-world ticket. She travelled throughout Australasia before settling in London—the perfect place to indulge her love of history and travel. For four years she lived and travelled throughout Europe before returning to her homeland. On the way back to Canada she stopped in Egypt, Jordan, Israel, India, Nepal, and of course, Australia and New Zealand. She lived again in Canada for one year before the lure of Europe and easy travel was too great and she returned to the UK.

Marriage and the birth of two babies later, she moved back to Canada to raise her children with her British husband. Two more children were born in Canada and her travel wings were well and truly clipped. Firmly rooted in the life of a stay-at-home mom, or trophy wife as she prefers to be called, she turned to writing to exercise her mind, travelling vicariously through her romance novels.

Her stories reflect her love of travel and feature locations as diverse as the wind-swept prairies of Canada to hot and humid cities in Asia. To discover other books written by Alexia or read her blog on inspirational destinations at https://alexia-adams.com or follow her on social media.

Facebook:
https://www.facebook.com/AlexiaAdamsAuthor/
Twitter: https://twitter.com/AlexiaAdamsAuth
Goodreads:
https://www.goodreads.com/author/show/706852
6.Alexia_Adams

Other Books by Alexia:

Love in Translation series:

Thailand with the Tycoon

Will being trapped in a failing resort change more than their itinerary?

When his older brother suffers a heart-attack, Caleb is sucked back into the family's virtually bankrupt hotel business. He reluctantly travels to Thailand to evaluate a last-chance resort with the help of a translator. Getting stranded with an enchanting local was not on the agenda. Neither was falling in love.

To read an excerpt visit https://alexia-adams.com

Bali with the Billionaire

He's all business. Until she makes him her business.

Ever since tragedy shattered Harrison Mackenzie's life, he's locked his passion away to focus on work. Until a captivating woman without boundaries crashes through his meticulously constructed barriers to reach the billionaire's broken heart. Is he finally ready to risk loving again?

To read an excerpt visit https://alexia-adams.com

Guide to Love series:

Miss Guided

Mystery writer Marcus Sullivan is determined find someone for his younger brother Liam. Playing matchmaker on holiday in St. Lucia, Marcus tries to interest Liam in a beautiful local tour guide Crescentia St. Ives. Then Marcus gets stranded with Crescentia and the plot to match her with his brother quickly incinerates in the flames of lust. No way can Liam have her when Marcus can't keep his hands off. Too bad he can't write a happier ending to their blossoming romance.

To read an excerpt https://alexia-adams.com

Played by the Billionaire

Internet security billionaire, Liam Manning, made a promise to his beloved brother, Marcus, to complete his mystery-romance manuscript. Problem is that Liam's experience with women is limited to the cold-hearted supermodels he usually dates. So falling back on his hacking skills, he infiltrates an online dating site to find a suitable woman to teach him about romance—regular guy style. What he didn't expect was for the feelings to be so … real. Can Liam finish the novel before Lorelei discovers his deceptions and, more critically, before she breaches the firewall around his heart?

To read an excerpt visit https://alexia-adams.com

His Billion-Dollar Dilemma

Simon Lamont is an ice-cold corporate pirate. But when he arrives in San Francisco to acquire a floundering company and is accosted by a cute engineer with fire in her eyes, it takes all Simon has to maintain his legendary cool. Helen will do whatever it takes to change his mind, and if that means becoming the sexy woman Simon didn't know he wanted, so be it. If only she wasn't about to walk into her own trap...

To read an excerpt visit https://alexia-adams.com

Masquerading with the Billionaire

World-renowned jewelry designer Remington Wolfe is competing for the commission of a lifetime and someone is trying to destroy his company from the inside. He's in for more than one surprise when his unexpected rescuer turns out to be a sexy computer specialist with a sharp tongue and even sharper mind.

To read an excerpt visit https://alexia-adams.com

Romance and Intrigue in the Greek Islands:

The Greek's Stowaway Bride

Hoping to make it to North Africa to free her uncle, heiress Rania Ghalli stows away on the yacht of Greek millionaire Demetri Christodoulou. But when Egyptian agents board the boat, she can either jump overboard … or claim she's Demetri's new bride. Demetri needs a wife to complete a land purchase so he agrees to play along—if she'll agree to a real marriage. But keeping the vivacious heiress out of his heart will be a lot harder than keeping her on his ship…

To read an excerpt visit https://alexia-adams.com

Romance in the Canadian Prairie:

Her Faux Fiancé

Take one fake engagement to a man she once loved, stir in a very real pregnancy, add a marriage of convenience, bake in the heat of revenge and you get the mess that has become Analise's life.

To read an excerpt visit https://alexia-adams.com

Daring to Love Again Series:

The Sicilian's Forgotten Wife

Bella Vanni has accepted that her presumed-dead husband is long gone, so it's a huge shock when he knocks on her door and announces his desire to resume their marriage. She can't trust his answers on where he's been or why he left, and she certainly isn't keen to walk away from the life she's constructed for herself in his absence. But when Matteo's freedom is threatened,

Bella must decide which is most important to her: everything she's painstakingly built or a second chance at a love that never died.

To read an excerpt visit https://alexia-adams.com

Business Trip Romance

Singapore Fling

Jeremy Lakewood is a bad boy gone good. Then he's sent on an extended business trip with the one woman who threatens everything he's worked so hard to achieve. Caught in the turmoil of remembered passion, will he have to choose the career that supports his widowed mother and disabled sister over the chance at a love to last a lifetime? When a series of startling revelations force these colleagues-with-benefits to reconsider their options, will love still be on the agenda?

To read an excerpt visit https://alexia-adams.com

An Inconvenient Series:

An Inconvenient Love

With the Italian economy in ruins, Luca Castellioni can't afford a distraction from running his successful property restoration company. However, he needs an English-speaking wife to cement a crucial deal. When his British bride-of-convenience undermines the foundations around his heart, he's forced to restructure his priorities. Is he too late for love?

To read an excerpt turn the page!

An Inconvenient Desire
Investment banker Jonathan Davis retreats to his Italian villa to lick his wounds following his divorce, so his flirtation with runway model Olivia Chapman is just that. But when his ex-wife dumps their toddler daughter on his doorstep, Olivia's assistance is a godsend that shakes up his world in more ways than one.

To read an excerpt visit https://alexia-adams.com

An Inconvenient Love

Chapter One

F2. Deal again.

The workday was endless when your biggest decision was FreeCell or solitaire. Today solitaire was the game of choice, and Sophia was already $830 down. Damn Vegas scoring. At least she didn't have to worry about anyone knocking at her door to collect that debt.

The front doorbell buzzed, and she switched the display on her monitor from the game to webcam. Metal chair legs scraping against the wood floor indicated that the elderly porter had been awakened from his nap and was on the way to answer the summons.

Look up, look up, she mentally willed the man standing at the door, waiting to be let in. Her telepathy not working, she tried adjusting the camera angle to get a better view, but all she could see was the top of his head. Dark hair, that was all. Useless angle, useless camera.

Not that she held out much hope that he would be worth looking at. The managing partner had mentioned as he passed her desk this morning that an important

Italian property developer was coming to meet with him. An image of a short, middle-aged man with a comb-over hairstyle came to her mind, and she suppressed a giggle.

The visitor eventually arrived at the reception area. A Georgian house didn't lend itself to the most efficient layout for an office. Trying to at least appear busy, Sophia pretended to save a document before turning to greet the man. She looked up, way up. Okay, so not short. And his black, slightly curly hair was brushed back from his face and fully covered his scalp. In fact, her fingers itched to run through it and release the curls further. His strong jaw and Roman nose looked like an advertisement for some amazing facial makeover. Dressed in a dark gray suit, he had an air of power. Even dressed more casually she was sure he would still have an aura of command.

This was no middle-aged specimen. The man standing before her was definitely in his prime. If he were a steer, he'd have AAA stamped on his left butt cheek, another image that left her battling the giggles. Until his dark eyes met hers, and all the air was sucked out of her lungs. He was so gorgeous, she clamped her lips together so she didn't accidently drool on her keyboard.

"Luca Castellioni to see Walter Bodman." His deep voice held only a hint of an Italian accent.

"Oh, yes, Mr. Castellioni. If you'd like to take a seat, I'll let Mr. Bodman know that you're here."

The guest smiled, as if distracted by a pleasant memory, and sat across the room in direct sight of her desk. Her suddenly nervous fingers had to twice dial the senior partner's secretary, and her voice came out all breathless when she announced the visitor.

"Mr. Bodman is just finishing up a conference call. He'll be down shortly." At least she managed to sound a little normal.

The enigmatic visitor acknowledged her statement and picked up a magazine from the table next to him. But every time she looked up, he was staring at her rather than reading. He made no effort to look away, and it was Sophia who broke the eye contact each time. She was sure he could hear her heartbeat pounding from across the room. The more she tried to ignore his presence, the more acutely she became aware of his every movement.

Walter Bodman's gruff voice booming across the room had never been so welcome. "Luca! Sorry to have kept you waiting. How wonderful to see you again. It's been what—three years?"

"Five," the Italian corrected. "You are doing well. Very nice offices…" His voice trailed away as he followed his host.

A sharp stab of pain made Sophia aware she'd been clenching her toes. She kicked off her sensible ballerina flats and dreamed for a moment of the handsome Italian massaging her feet. There was no way she was going to be able to go back to her game of solitaire now.

Her mobile phone vibrated on the desk beside her. The bank was kindly advising that her account was now down to fourteen pounds fifty pence, and still six days to payday. With the tuition due for the next term of her interior design studies, her finances wouldn't be much better even after she was paid.

She logged on to a job finder website, but there wasn't much call for a receptionist with minimal experience and no real desire to do the job. And none paid more than what she was making now. Her desk phone buzzed, and she shut down the webpage. Might as well do the job she had, rather than worry about the one she couldn't get.

An hour later Sophia was transcribing a letter one of the secretaries sent down when a shadow crossed her screen and the hair on the back of her neck stood on end. A hint of sandalwood and citrus tickled her nose. Looking up, she wasn't surprised to see the Italian businessman standing at her desk.

"I look forward to seeing you tonight, Miss Stevens."

"I … ah … I … how do you know my name?" She latched onto the first thing that came to mind while she tried to make sense of his words.

He pointed at the small plaque on her desk with her name inscribed. "Walter has invited me to the company party. I hope we will have the opportunity to talk. Until tonight…" Turning on his heel, he strode from the room.

Why would a gorgeous Italian millionaire want to talk to me? Her toes curled again.

• • •

Luca entered the marquee in St. James's Square and searched for Walter. At least that's what his brain told his eyes to look for. They decided to hunt down the blonde receptionist instead. She was beautiful. But he knew lots of beautiful women. Maybe it was the laughter in her green eyes or the way she'd tried not to notice him that intrigued him. Whatever it was, he couldn't relax until he spotted her.

She stood twenty meters away, chatting with a couple of other women, a glass of champagne in her hand. Her simple black dress was elegant and alluring, hugging her curves rather than pushing them up for all to see. His pulse quickened, as it had when he had seen her in the office. Before he could approach her, Walter's over-loud voice stopped him.

"Luca, glad you could join us. I want to introduce you to Chet Wilkins, an American business acquaintance. He's scouting new locations for his boutique hotel chain. He's looking for rural properties to turn into luxury spas where stressed executives can go to relax. But I'll let him tell you all the requirements."

Walter led him to a tall, thin man in his early sixties, standing beside a woman of similar age who was wearing too little dress and too much makeup. Luca glanced to where Sophia had been chatting, only to find she was no longer with the group of women. Forcing his mind back to business, he smiled at the American couple.

Thirty minutes later, his smile was strained and he shifted another couple centimeters away from Mrs. Leslie Wilkins. She stood so close, he was in danger of suffocating on her cloying perfume. And he was pretty damn sure it wasn't by accident she kept brushing his thigh or backside with her hand. Her husband continued to drone on about the ideal properties he was looking for, completely ignoring his wife. Walter had excused himself ten minutes ago, so it was just the three of them, penned into a corner. A waiter passed and Leslie grabbed yet another glass of champagne.

"Luca, there you are. I wondered where you'd got to." The sexy voice of Walter's receptionist halted the glass halfway to the American woman's lips. Sophia's small hand slipped into his, and he gave it a squeeze of appreciation.

He glanced down at her upturned face and had to stop himself from bending down and kissing her slightly parted lips. Sophia did weird things to his self-control. He was probably in more danger from her than Leslie Wilkins. "My apologies, *amore*. Walter introduced me to Mr. and Mrs. Wilkins, and we got so engrossed in our conversation, I lost track of time. Leslie, Chet, do you know Sophia Stevens?"

Leslie Wilkins downed half the glass of champagne in one go and turned to her husband. "I'm going to get something to eat," she said before walking away, her steps wobbly.

"Nice to see you again, Mr. Wilkins. Pardon me, I didn't mean to interrupt your conversation," Sophia added. "I'll make sure Mrs. Wilkins finds the buffet okay."

As quietly as she'd arrived, Sophia left, a light, lingering scent of fresh fruit and an odd tingle in his palm the only remnants of her appearance. Without missing a beat, Chet Wilkins continued his property wish list.

"I know of three properties that would suit your

needs. When will you be in Italy?" As much as he'd love to cement a relationship with Chet, he couldn't keep his mind off Sophia. Maybe she'd been checking him out and noticed his discomfort? His breath caught in his chest. What other hidden talents did the beguiling receptionist possess?

Chet's voice interrupted his contemplations. "We'll be there in about six weeks. My wife is accompanying me."

Luca took a sip of his drink to expunge the bad taste in his mouth at the thought of more time in the company of Leslie Wilkins. "Here's my card. Call me when you firm up your plans. I believe we can enjoy a mutually beneficial business partnership."

Chet Wilkins pocketed his card and shook hands. "I look forward to working with you. Guess I'd better round up Leslie," he said, then wandered toward the bar area rather than the buffet. Apparently, the man knew exactly where he'd find his wife.

Luca scanned the crowd, ignoring the open invitation on several of the women's faces. Eventually he found Sophia, standing alone by the ice sculpture. The tiny white lights strung through the marquee danced off her golden hair, drawing him like a moth to a flame.

"Thank you," he said, resisting the urge to take her hand again, to see if the connection he'd experienced earlier had been real.

A hesitant smile played about her lips. "I wasn't rescuing you. I was saving Chet Wilkins. He was getting more embarrassed each time she touched you. Mr. Wilkins is a nice man; he's been to the office several times. I didn't like watching his wife flirt with someone in front of him."

Damn, she hadn't been checking him out. He had to force a smile. "Well, whatever your motive, I am grateful. Can I get you another drink?" He glanced down at her hand; the champagne was still at the same level it had been when he'd first seen her almost forty-five minutes ago.

"No, I'm good. Don't let me detain you. I'm sure there must be other important people here you'd like to talk with."

Was she trying to get rid of him? She'd met his gaze briefly before staring at his left shoulder. "Why do you feel you are not important?"

"I'm the receptionist." She shrugged, her gaze only flicking to his momentarily.

"Receptionists are the first introduction to a company. They are vital in portraying the correct image. You should never think less of yourself."

"It's only a job."

"Well if you could be anything you wanted, what would it be?"

"A ninja." This time her eyes did meet his and the laughter was back in their green depths.

Whether it was the audacity of her reply or her smile he wasn't sure, but he sucked in a deep breath. "An interesting career choice. Why would you like to be a ninja?"

"Black's my favorite color." Her flippant answer made him smile.

"So what is holding you back? A lack of black

outfits?"

She laughed. "Ah, if only. No, the best ninja schools are in Japan, and I don't have a passport." She shrugged and looked once again over his shoulder.

"Am I keeping you from someone? Your husband or boyfriend?" He'd noticed in the office she didn't wear a ring, and there had been no photos on her desk. But that didn't mean she wasn't involved with someone. He repressed the disappointment that swept through him.

"No, I'm here alone. I only came because Mr. Bodman insisted everyone in the company attend. But I think I've stayed long enough. I see Mr. Wilkins steering his wife toward the exit, so you should be safe now."

"Safe, thanks to you. In fact your timely intervention has given me an idea. Will you meet me tomorrow? I have an opportunity I would like to discuss with you."

"You need an untrained ninja to protect you?"

"Something like that."

Sophia tilted her head to one side and stared at him. Finally she shrugged her delicate shoulders again. "I usually take a walk around St. James's Park at lunchtime. I'll be on the bridge at 12:30 if you still want to talk with me." She spoke as though she didn't really believe he would show up.

"Tomorrow at 12:30 then."

Her eyes searched his face but he kept his expression carefully neutral. If she discovered his interest, she may not come. The plan that had started when she slipped her hand into his had solidified with their brief conversation. Yes, Sophia Stevens would do very nicely.

. . .

Sophia stood on the bridge and looked out over the lake to the fountain and Buckingham Palace in the background. Spring had come early; the trees were in bloom and crocuses and daffodils soaked up the sunshine. To stop from searching for Luca, she stared at the ducks. A male mallard was enticing a female with a display of his bright plumage. She wished she were a duck. They didn't worry about paying the rent or putting their brother through college.

She should have brought some water to drink. Her mouth was so dry, she may not be able to talk. If he came. Having tossed and turned half the night, she'd finally reached the conclusion that Luca must be opening an office in London and wanted to employ her. Then she'd spent the rest of the night working out exactly how much salary she could reasonably request. If she asked for too much, he'd think her greedy. If she asked for too little, she'd be a drone for the rest of her life, never achieving her dream of her own interior design company.

The question she hadn't been able to answer was whether she could actually work for him. She'd been unable to concentrate when he sat across from her in the office. And then last night at the party she could barely meet his gaze, sure he'd be able to see through her veil of bravado to the frightened girl inside.

Lost in her problems, she didn't notice Luca

approach until his arm brushed hers on the bridge rail. She took a deep, calming breath. Her mouth suddenly started to salivate, and his intoxicating aftershave lured her to lean closer. He'd come.

"I am pleased to see you again." Perhaps it was her imagination, but his accent seemed thicker today. He was immaculate, not a hair out of place, his suit undoubtedly costing more than she made all month. He was way beyond her league. What else could he want except a receptionist?

"You said you had a job opportunity to discuss with me." She moved her arm away so they no longer touched. What was he playing at? Did he think because she'd slipped her hand into his at the party that she was available for an affair? Well, if so, he'd find out soon enough she wasn't going to sleep with him just because he was rich, and powerful, and gorgeous.

"An opportunity, yes. As you know, I own a property development and restoration company in the north of Italy, based in Milan." His low voice, so close, sounded like they were sharing an illicit secret. "I am now in a position to sign some large contracts with British and American companies, like Chet Wilkins. However, my secretary, who is very good, does not speak fluent English. I cannot afford to have misunderstandings."

Excitement raced through her. It was a job offer. And from the sound of it, based in Italy. She was tired of London. Tired of working two, sometimes three, jobs just to make ends meet, never getting ahead. A move to Italy would be the change she longed for, a chance to escape the constant reminders of her horrific past. Before she could respond however, he continued.

"I need more than just an English-speaking secretary. I have reached a point in my life where all my business associates are married, and new clients are always asking about my personal life. It seems to disconcert them when I say I am unmarried, and it is becoming a hindrance to my success. Family is very important in Italy. It is seen as a sign of stability. However, my entire focus at the moment is on building my business. I do not have the time now, or in the foreseeable future, to romance a woman. Besides, a wife who loved me would expect me to be home every night and probably feel neglected with the amount of time I spend working."

Sophia struggled to keep her face neutral and not let her puzzlement show. Why was he talking about his need for a wife?

"Last night at the party you proved to me you are able to read a situation and act appropriately. I also believe you are good at your job. Walter is an astute man; he would not have kept you employed if you were not a hard worker." He leaned toward her. His voice had dropped even more, and she wondered where he was going with this so-called opportunity.

"I think, therefore, that I should align my requirements and seek an English wife. One who would be able to assist me in my business, and also provide the home life expected of a man in my position. Are you interested?" He turned to her, his eyes sweeping over her face, awaiting her response. His smile held a hint of warmth, but his eyes were guarded, as though there was something he wasn't telling. Something that prompted him to ask her, of all people.

This was it. She'd finally snapped. Her brain had imploded from worry and boredom, and as a result she was fantasizing about marriage proposals and being swept away to live in a castle in Italy. At this point she should reach into her pocket and pull out the other glass slipper. Except the only thing in her pocket was lint. And the only romance in her life was in the books she read. Maybe Luca was the one having a meltdown? She searched his face for some sign of insanity.

He looked serious. The contents of her stomach shifted. The man had actually just proposed to her. "Mr. Castellioni, I'm sure there's a long line of suitable women who would love to marry you. We only met yesterday. And as I told you at the party, I'm just a receptionist."

"You called me Luca last evening. What has changed?"

Aside from one of them going completely insane? Him for proposing … or her for actually considering it and not walking away.

"Last night was for show, to help Mr. Wilkins. This is…"

"This is between us. I can assure you there is no other woman I would consider marrying. I realize it may seem absurd to speak of marriage when we have recently met. You said last night you were alone. Did I misunderstand? Are you in a relationship?"

"No, no, I'm not involved with anyone. But that

doesn't mean I am going to run off and marry the first man who asks me," she replied. *Even if he is incredibly gorgeous. What kind of man offers marriage to a complete stranger? One who considered marriage a business arrangement, obviously. Could I do the same?*

"You do not have to give me an answer now. Have dinner with me tonight, and we can get to know each other. I would appreciate, though, if you would keep this discussion between us." He leaned forward again and there was an intensity in his dark eyes but a warmth, too, a banked passion that both unsettled and intrigued her.

Dazed, she agreed to meet him again at Quaglino's. Sophia didn't even ask how he had managed to get a table at a restaurant that was usually booked a month in advance. She was sure if he just showed up, the maître d' would lose someone else's reservation in order to accommodate him. If he expected her to bow to his every desire he was in for a shock. Sophia Stevens was no man's doormat. But she wasn't about to reject him without discovering exactly what he wanted.

And what she could get out of the deal.

~~~

Get your copy of **An Inconvenient Love** *today!*